About the Autho

Simon Bywater's journey bega
was born into a bustling hous
unfolded amidst the rustic ch
Cambridgeshire. His family's
upbringing, with a father haili
a mother rooted in Luton, Bedfordshire.

At the age of sixteen, Simon embarked on a remarkable path by joining the Royal Marine Commandos in 1985. Over the years, he served with 40 Commando RM, traversing the globe, and facing the challenges of active service, including a significant stint in Northern Iraq during Operation Safe Haven in 1991. Simon's tenure in the Marines instilled in him a profound sense of duty and resilience that would shape his future endeavors.

Transitioning from military life, Simon embarked on a new chapter by joining Greater Manchester Police. In roles spanning Uniform and the Criminal Investigation Department (CID), he gained invaluable experience in the vibrant communities of Wythenshawe and Moss Side, South Manchester. However, Simon's roots beckoned him back to Cambridgeshire, and at the dawn of the Millennium, he returned with his family to embrace a new chapter.

Driven by an entrepreneurial spirit, Simon ventured into the realm of business, where he found success through various ventures. Yet, his ambitions extended beyond commerce. Simon's multifaceted journey saw him delve into the realm of literature, where he is currently engrossed in crafting new works. Additionally, his dedication to public service is evident through his roles as an elected Cambridgeshire County Councillor and Huntingdonshire District Councillor, where he tirelessly advocates for his community's interests.

Beyond his professional pursuits, Simon finds solace and vitality in his personal passions. Through his diverse interests and unwavering commitment, Simon Bywater embodies a spirit of resilience, adaptability, and boundless curiosity.

BY SIMON BYWATER

Forced Out

Honourable Retribution

PAYBACK "When life costs"

Life Skills for Young People and How to
Become a Decent Human Being

Verses of Life

SIMON BYWATER

" WINTERS LINE: HELIX PROTOCOL"

A FATHER'S SECRETS. A SON'S WAR. A SYSTEM BUILT TO DESTROY BOTH.

Prologue

The frigid air cut through Nikolia's threadbare jacket like a knife, sending shivers down his spine as he huddled against the icy wind. Around him, the desolate expanse of eastern Ukraine stretched out in all directions, a barren wasteland of snow-covered fields and skeletal trees stripped bare by the harsh winter weather. The once lush and verdant wooded areas lay in ruin, their once majestic trees now nothing more than splintered remnants of their former selves. Repeated explosions had torn through the forest like a relentless force of nature, leaving behind a landscape of devastation and desolation. The ground was littered with debris, making it treacherous to move and walk. Jagged branches jutted out at odd angles, their sharp edges gleaming ominously in the dim light. Every step was a gamble, a perilous dance with danger as hidden obstacles lurked beneath the fallen foliage. The air was thick with the acrid scent of smoke and charred wood, a grim reminder of the violence that had torn through this once tranquil sanctuary. And in the chaos and destruction, the sound of distant explosions echoed like thunder in the distance, a constant reminder of the ever-present threat that loomed. It was a landscape devoid of life, save for the weary souls who trudged through its frozen depths, their faces etched with the weariness of endless conflict.

Nikolia was one of them, a young Russian conscript torn from the warmth and safety of home and thrust into the heart of a war he never asked for. With each step he took, he could feel the weight of his burden pressing down upon him, a heavy mantle of responsibility that threatened to crush him beneath its onerous weight. Yet, despite the overwhelming odds stacked against him, he refused to surrender to its despair.

Every day was a battle for survival, a relentless struggle against a determined enemy and the brutal winter weather that sought to claim him as its own. In the trenches and foxholes that dotted the front lines, Nikolia fought alongside other young Russian conscripts who, like him, had been conscripted into service against their will. They were brothers in arms, bound together by the shared experience of war and the desperate desire to make it home alive. One thing was clear they hated this wasted war.

Amongst the twisting trenches that snaked through the scarred earth, there was a palpable sense of scarcity, a stark absence of the supplies that were vital for survival on the front lines. Food was scarce, and what little remained was often meagre and unappetising, stretching thin to feed the hungry mouths of weary soldiers. Ammunition, too, was in short supply, with every bullet and shell precious beyond measure, hoarded like rare treasure in the face of relentless enemy advances. Foraging off the dead and wounded comrades was commonplace for survival.

The harsh realities of the frontline were doubled by the relentless onslaught of Ukrainian forces, who seemed to possess an uncanny ability to disrupt supply lines and cut off their crucial lifelines. Their relentless attacks left the soldiers stranded, isolated in their muddy fortresses with little hope of respite or reinforcement. Sitting in a cold, wet trench in Ukraine breeds a fear that crawls deep into the bones, a fear that wraps around the heart with icy fingers.

But it's not just the biting cold that sends shivers down the spine; it's the ever-present threat from drones hovering overhead, their mechanical eyes scanning the desolate landscape below. Each buzzing sound sends a jolt of terror through the soldiers, their nerves stretched taut like the wires of a tripwire.

Every moment feels precarious, as if the sky itself might rain down destruction at any second. During such uncertainty, fear becomes a constant companion, whispering its sinister warnings with each gust of wind and each distant hum of a drone.

For Nikolia and his comrades, each passing day brought with it a new level of desperation, a desperate struggle not only against the enemy forces that pressed ever closer but also against the harsh realities of hunger and deprivation. Yet, despite the odds stacked against them, they refused to yield, clinging to the flickering flame of hope of survival in this hell and an end would come soon.

Within this chaos and carnage of the battlefield, Nikolia's thoughts often drifted to the safety and comfort of home, to the warmth of his mother's embrace and the laughter of his friends. He longed for the simple pleasures of life, the taste of hot food, the feel of clean clothes against his skin, the sound of music drifting through the air. Yet, such luxuries were but distant memories, lost to the ravages of war and the passage of time.

Nikolia's heart seethed with a bitter resentment, a simmering anger that threatened to boil over at any moment. He detested every aspect of the war, detested the senseless violence, the needless bloodshed, and the cruel twist of fate that had conscripted him into this living nightmare. But above all, he detested the oppressive regime of the Socialist Putin-led Russian government, whose iron grip extended even into the depths of his own soul.

For Nikolia, conscription was not just a violation of his freedom, it was an assault on his very identity, a betrayal of everything he held dear. Raised on the ideals of liberty and democracy, he had never imagined that he would one day find himself at the mercy of a government that sought to crush dissent and silence opposition with an iron fist.

But as he stood on the front lines, surrounded by the deafening roar of gunfire and the stench of death, Nikolia knew that he had no choice but to fight. The weight of his rifle felt like a massive burden in his hands, a grim reminder of the heavy toll that war exacted upon the vulnerable young human soul. Yet, despite his revulsion at the thought of taking another life, he knew that he could not afford to show weakness, not in a world where the slightest hesitation meant certain death.

With a heavy heart and determined resolve, Nikolia steeled himself for the battles that lay ahead. He would fight not for glory or honour, but for his own survival, for the chance to one day return to the world he had left behind, and to reclaim the freedom that had been stolen from him. Nikolia vowed to never lose sight of the flame of hope that burned within him in the darkness of war.

His only lifeline to the outside world was a secure phone provided by his father, a slender thread of connection that stretched across the vast expanse of distance and despair. Through terse text messages exchanged in the dead of night, Nikolia clung to the hope of escape, desperate to find a way back to the safety and freedom of the West. Each message was a lifeline, a reminder that he was not alone, that somewhere out there, someone was fighting for him.

Despite his deep-seated desire to escape the horrors of war, Nikolai found himself trapped in a cruel paradox. The thought of surrendering to the Ukrainians lingered in his mind like a tantalising whisper of freedom, a glimmer of hope in the chaos and despair.

But the harsh reality of the battlefield offered no guarantees, no assurances of safety or protection. Every moment spent contemplating surrender was fraught with peril, a gamble with his very life hanging in the balance. For Nikolai, the fear of being shot by either the enemy or his own side loomed large, casting a shadow of doubt over any fleeting thoughts of escape. And so, he remained bound by the chains of war, his dreams of freedom tempered by the harsh realities of survival.

Chapter 1: Ghosts of Canal Street

In the underbelly of a city that never really slept, where cheap neon bled into rain-streaked concrete and the past whispered from every broken window, Alex Winters moved like a man who belonged to none of it yet knew it all too well.

He stood just over six feet, broad-shouldered but lean, built from years of hard living, harder training, and the slow reconstruction of a life once shattered. His brown hair was cropped short and often hidden beneath a hood or cap. Faint scars lined his knuckles, and a jagged one traced along his right temple, a souvenir from a roadside bomb in another country, another life.

His face told stories he never would, quiet stories, brutal stories. Tired eyes, once a piercing grey, now dulled by years of sleepless nights and too many regrets. He didn't move like a civilian. There was control in his walk, a deliberate grace honed from combat and caution. But there was something fractured behind that stillness a man who'd seen too much, lost too much, and carried it all in silence.

Alex was, above all else, a man rebuilding. Brick by brick. Fight by fight.

He walked alone beneath the skeletal outlines of scaffolding and old red-brick warehouses, hands shoved deep into his jacket pockets, head down but eyes always scanning. Not for danger. Not tonight.

For peace.

It never came.

The sickly glow of kebab shops and mini markets flickered behind grimy windows, casting patchwork shadows across the puddles. Somewhere a bottle smashed. Laughter, coarse and hollow, rang out from a side street.

And further down the alley, the faint hum of a distant train, relentless and indifferent, like time itself.

Alex turned into Canal Street, not for pleasure, but habit. Every addict has their circuits, and this was once his. The alley stank of piss and old beer. A rat skittered beneath a skip. He pulled a cigarette from his coat pocket with trembling fingers, lit it with a half-dead Bic, and sucked in deeply not for the nicotine, but for the illusion of control.

The tremor in his hand betrayed him anyway.

Nineteen months clean. No relapses. Not yet. But some nights, nights like this, the line blurred between progress and purgatory.

His phone buzzed.

A message from Megan, the sponsor he rarely replied to:

"Still proud of you. Just one day at a time."

Alex ignored it. Not because he didn't care, but because he did. Too much. He couldn't let anyone in. Not really. They always left. Or worse, they stayed long enough to see what was broken.

He now worked at a car parts distribution warehouse near Trafford a big come down from his days in special forces. Nights mostly. Inventory, logistics, the odd argument with a late delivery driver. It wasn't glamorous. It wasn't fulfilling.

But it was safe.

A place where no one asked too many questions. Where the past stayed in the past, sealed away behind industrial roller doors and the scent of oil and rubber.

Still, it wasn't enough.

He'd felt it building again, that itch under the skin. The pull of chaos disguised as comfort. The whispers of old ghosts: Afghan, Iraq, some God-forsaken checkpoint outside Mosul. And worse still his father's voice, gravelled and cold, telling him to straighten up, to endure, to be more than his pain.

That voice had gone quiet years ago.

But lately, in the dead space between sleep and waking, it had come back.

To fight the pull, Alex had found his own arsenal not bullets or gear, but routine. The gym had become his battlefield. Steel, sweat, silence.

Each morning, after his shift, he hit the weights at a crumbling boxing gym above an old social club off Princess Parkway. It smelled like liniment and aggression, but it was real. No mirrors. No influencers. Just work.

He trained like a man with something to prove, not to the world, but to himself. Heavy bag. Squats. Sprints. No shortcuts. No excuses.

And with that, a new rhythm emerged: cook, work, train, sleep, repeat.

He stopped drinking. Swapped Red Bulls and kebabs for chicken, quinoa, and spinach. Started reading again, not just crime thrillers and soldier memoirs, but real things: psychology, Stoicism, philosophy, books about trauma, life, forgiveness and fate.

Little by little, he clawed his way back from the edge.

People started to notice.

The guys at the warehouse stopped calling him "Ghost."

His foreman gave him more responsibility.

Even the woman at the corner shop smiled at him differently.

But deep down, Alex knew the truth.

He was still waiting. Waiting for something to pull him forward or drag him back.

Because even after all this progress the clear eyes, the cleaner blood, the steadier hands there was a sense of unfinished business pressing at the edges of his soul.

Not just addiction. Not just war. But something older. Deeper.

Something tied to the father he hadn't spoken to in over a decade. The man who had raised him like a soldier, then vanished into the silence. John Winters.

Alex never knew whether his father was proud of him. Or disappointed. Or simply gone. It didn't matter now.

Until that night.

3:09 AM

As he passed under the old canal bridge, his phone buzzed again not a text, but a call.

Unknown number.

International code. Ukrainian.

He hesitated. Stared at the screen.

Then answered.

"Yeah?"

A silence.

Then, a voice. Rough. Ukrainian accent. Urgent.

"You don't know me. But you need to go home"

The call then finished as quickly as it had started.

Chapter 2: The Knock

The rain tapped steadily against the single-pane window of Alex Winters' flat, painting slow-moving rivulets across the glass as the dull orange glow of the streetlight filtered through. The air inside was heavy, not with smoke or clutter, but with that quiet weight of someone who'd spent years learning how to sit still in discomfort.

Alex sat slouched on his threadbare sofa, a chipped mug of cold coffee cradled in his hands. The cushions were tired, the carpet worn smooth in two distinct paths from pacing. The walls were nicotine-stained relics of another tenant's life, but he hadn't got round to painting over them. He liked their honesty, scarred, stained, but still standing.

He wore joggers and a plain grey hoodie that clung to his lean frame. His build was tight with the kind of strength earned from reps, sweat, and discipline, not vanity. Tattoos peeked from the cuffs of his sleeves, remnants of a younger, more volatile self. His dark hair was longer than regulation but well-kept, and the stubble on his jaw was deliberate, not lazy. His eyes pale steel, always alert, scanned the room absently, like they didn't trust the silence.

Alex had the look of a man who knew how to break something and how to fix it but preferred not to do either. Stillness, to him, was effort.

It had been months since he'd last used. The cravings had gone but never really died. They just changed their shape, turned into restlessness, bad dreams, the gnawing suspicion that redemption might not come for men like him. And tonight, the world felt too quiet. Like something was circling.

Then came the knock.

Not loud. Not rushed. Just three deliberate taps.

He tensed, placing the mug down slowly, listening.

A second knock followed. Firmer this time. Closer.

Alex crossed the room in silence, boots soft against the scuffed laminate floor. He paused by the door, heart thudding once like a warning bell.

He didn't expect visitors. Not this late. Not ever.

With one hand on the lock, he opened it.

The corridor outside was dim, but the figure standing beneath the flickering overhead bulb was unmistakable.

"Alex," came the voice, roughened by time, tinged with regret. "We need to talk."

Alex's breath caught in his throat.

Standing in the threshold was John Winters. His father.

The man who had vanished without explanation. Who left him with a house full of silence and a head full of unanswered questions.

Alex didn't speak. He simply stared, trying to reconcile the flesh-and-blood man before him with the ghost he'd been resenting for over a decade.

John looked older. Silver streaked through the hair above his ears, and deep creases framed his eyes. But he stood tall, shoulders squared, wearing the stillness of a man used to waiting in dangerous places. He wore a dark coat, simple but tailored, and his boots looked far too clean for someone who just wandered into this part of Manchester.

"What do you want, Dad?" Alex asked, voice clipped, bitter.

John stepped forward a little, but not over the threshold. "I know I don't deserve your forgiveness. But there are things you need to know." Alex said nothing. The door remained half-open, the flat behind him unchanged, lived-in, stripped down, carefully protected from emotion.

John met his son's eyes, his voice low. "You need to understand… there's more to our family than you know."

Alex crossed his arms. "Right. That's why you disappeared for fourteen years because of family loyalty."

John's jaw tightened, but he didn't flinch. "I was never just a businessman, Alex. I worked for an intelligence unit, off-books. Covert. Most of what we did never made it into any report."

Alex raised an eyebrow, the sarcasm barely concealed. "So, what, you were 007 while I was skipping school and watching Mum try not to cry at the kitchen sink?"

John looked away for a moment, as if bracing against something internal. Then back. "I'm telling you now because time's running out. There are forces at play, and they're moving quickly. And whether you believe me or not, your names already involved."

"You didn't come here to apologise," Alex muttered, stepping aside finally. "You came because you need something."

John walked in slowly, glancing around the small flat with quiet calculation. He didn't comment on the decor or the size. He simply took in the details like a man scanning a map. A fading photograph of Alex and his mum at Blackpool, smiling despite the wind and cheap camera flash sat on the windowsill.

"There's a lot I kept from you," he said, voice quieter now. "Too much. But there's one truth I can't keep anymore". John sat, but not comfortably. He perched, tense. Like a man waiting for the verdict before the trial had even begun.

"You have a half-brother."

Alex blinked. "What?"

John nodded. "His name's Nikolai. He's younger than you. Russian mother. Born during an assignment I ran "back in the day". I tried to protect him. Tried to keep his name buried."

"Jesus Christ…" Alex turned away, dragging a hand through his hair. "What is this, some kind of spy soap opera?"

John continued, undeterred. "Nikolai's been conscripted. Russian army. They've sent him to Ukraine. Frontline. He's in real danger and he has no idea who I really am."

Alex turned back slowly. "And you want to go get him."

"I'm going," John said firmly. "But I can't do it alone."

Silence stretched between them.

The rain outside thickened, masking the city in a dull, relentless hiss.

"I'm not who I used to be," Alex finally said, voice low. "I'm not you. I'm not trained for war anymore. I stack brake pads in a warehouse and drink chamomile tea to sleep."

"I know who you are," John said, his gaze steady. "And I know what you're capable of. You just forgot."

Alex swallowed hard. Part of him wanted to throw his father out. Slam the door. Burn whatever bridge had just been halfway built.

But there was something in John's voice. A flicker of urgency. A strange tone of fear.

And buried beneath his own resentment, something old stirred. A pull. Not toward the man in his flat, but toward something that felt unfinished.

For a long moment, the silence was deafening.

Alex leaned forward, his voice low. "You had another son. A secret life. And you just… kept it quiet?"

"I was still married to your mother," John said. "You were still young. She didn't know. When she passed"

"Don't," Alex cut in, sharply. "Don't drag her into this."

John nodded once, slowly. "I wanted to protect you. Both of you. I thought… separating my lives was the only way."

Alex gave a bitter laugh and rose to his feet, pacing toward the kitchenette. "You thought compartmentalising people was easier than telling the truth."

"I thought it was safer."

"For whom?" Alex spun around, eyes blazing. "Because it sure as hell wasn't for me. You vanished, left Mum to explain your absence, your silences. And now you show up with Cold War leftovers and some brother I never knew existed?"

John said nothing for a moment, then reached into his coat pocket and pulled out a creased photograph. He placed it on the coffee table.

A boy, maybe ten, dark-eyed, sharp-featured, standing beside a woman outside a crumbling Soviet-era building. The resemblance was distant but undeniable, in the brow, the stance, the tension in the shoulders.

Alex stared down at it, breathing hard.

John's voice was quieter now. "I lost contact with Lena years ago. Everything went dark after she disappeared. It took me years to track Nikolai down. Turns out, he's been conscripted. Russian army. Sent to the Donetsk front."

Alex stared harder at the photo, like it might yield more answers if he looked long enough.

"Christ," he muttered. "He's just a kid."

They're using him like cannon fodder. No choice, no training."

Alex ran a hand down his face. "Why tell me this now?"

John looked him square in the eye. "Because I'm going to get him out."

A long pause.

"You want me to come with you."

"I do."

Alex laughed, short and hollow. "I've spent two years trying to keep my head above water. Staying clean. Working. Finally getting some normal purpose back. And now you want me to dive headfirst into a warzone for someone I've never met?"

"I'm not dragging you. You have a choice. But I came to you because I trust you more than anyone else."

"That's rich."

John didn't react. Just nodded, slowly. "I've got contacts. Ukrainian side. Some of them still remember me. They'll help. But it's a tight window. After that, Nikolai's unit is redeployed. He won't survive the next rotation."

Alex didn't say anything. He stared at the photograph again.

A brother.

A stranger.

His father's sins printed in pixels.

"You really think you can find him? Extract him?"

"I wouldn't have come here if I didn't."

Alex paced again, then stopped by the window, looking out over the wet rooftops. The city seemed quiet, indifferent. But under it all, like a second heartbeat, was the sound of something turning. Something inevitable.

"I've spent my whole life resenting you," Alex said finally. "For disappearing. For letting her die alone. For turning your back on all of us."

John didn't speak.

"But this?" Alex said. "This I get. Not the lies. Not the excuses. But saving someone who doesn't deserve to be there."

He turned.

"I'm in. But this time, you tell me everything."

John nodded, standing. "Deal."

Alex picked up the photo and tucked it into a drawer.

Whatever happened next, this time, he wasn't going to be in the dark.

And for the first time in a long time, the quiet in the room felt different.

It wasn't peace.

But it wasn't silence, either.

It was the sound of old ghosts preparing to walk again.

Chapter 3: Into the Unknown

John Winters had spent a lifetime living in the grey.

His world had never been one of clear lines or clean endings. It was built on half-truths, burned identities, and silent compromises. Even those closest to him, including his wife, and later his son had only ever seen a shadow of the man behind the passport.

For decades, he'd slipped through borders and backrooms with practiced ease, whispering names in one city, disappearing into another. Moscow. Tbilisi. Ankara. Berlin. Always two steps ahead. Always disposable. He'd mastered the art of compartmentalisation, file away the lies, bury the regrets.

But there was one thing he had never been able to bury.

Nikolai.

A boy born not just out of passion, but out of fracture, from a mission that blurred into something human in a place no one was supposed to care. Lena had been sharp and principled, a translator with more intelligence than most of the handlers John had ever worked with. They'd survived months of chaos together in the dying days of the Soviet bloc. She had known exactly who he was and what would happen when he left.

He hadn't meant to stay. He certainly hadn't meant to love her.

But the boy had changed everything.

Now that boy, his son was a uniformed ghost on the Russian frontlines, caught in a war he didn't believe in, on a side that didn't even know his name.

John stood in Alex's kitchen, his back to the counter, staring down at the encrypted phone in his hand.

The latest intel had just come through. Nikolai's unit had moved again farther West. A meat grinder sector.

They were running out of time.

"We have to go to Ukraine," John said, his voice low but certain.

Alex looked up from where he sat, elbows on the kitchen table, the photograph of Nikolai still beside him. "That's what I thought you were going to say."

John nodded. "We need to find him. And get him out. Across the lines, across the border… home."

Alex leaned back in the chair and rubbed his temples. "You say that like it's a weekend job. But this isn't like some black-bag op in Serbia, is it? This is a warzone. Full-blown artillery. Occupied cities. Satellite surveillance. And you're what, pushing sixty?"

John cracked a half-smile. "Sixty-two. Still faster than most of the lads they send in now."

Alex didn't laugh. His brow furrowed with concern. "You realise how insane this sounds, right?"

"Of course. But we've both seen worse."

Alex gave a short exhale through his nose. "I haven't."

John studied him for a moment, then sat opposite. "You've fought your own wars. Just different ones."

That silenced the room for a beat.

Alex glanced at the photo again. "He looks… like you. But younger. Harder around the eyes."

"He's had to be," John murmured. "He hasn't seen me in years". I don't think he was ever really told about me as a child."

Alex shook his head slowly. "So, this is the plan. Find a stranger in the middle of a warzone who doesn't know who you are, who might not even want saving, and try to get him out without either of us getting killed."

John held his gaze. "Yes."

A long pause stretched between them.

Alex finally said, "How?"

"I've got people in Kyiv," John replied. "Two old handlers still in the game, freelance now, but they know the routes. I've arranged contact. But to reach them, we need to cross through Kraków first, then overland into Lviv. Safer that way. Official flights are out, too much scrutiny."

"And you've got passports?"

"Better. Clean docs. No links. MI6 never burned all my old assets."

Alex scoffed. "You're a walking Cold War relic."

"I'm a survivor," John said simply.

Alex stood, restless now. "And how the hell are we going to afford this? Travel, equipment, bribes I can barely afford my rent."

John reached into his duffel and unzipped a side compartment. He pulled out a weathered cash belt and laid it on the table. Bundles of euros and dollars wrapped and marked.

Alex blinked. "That real?"

"Some things never go out of style," John said. "This is enough to move quiet and fast. Enough to grease whatever wheels need turning."

Alex sat back down. There was no denying the gravity of it anymore. It wasn't just a wild story or a photo on a table. This was happening.

He looked at the cash. Then at his father.

"And if we get caught?"

"Then we adapt. Like we always do."

Alex looked away. The question that had been simmering finally spilled out: "Why me? After all these years? After everything?"

John hesitated. "Because you're the only one I trust. And because you're stronger than you think."

Alex swallowed hard. His mind was racing, the danger, the cost, the years of absence and resentment but beneath it all, there was something undeniable. A name. A face. A bond, however buried.

And a boy, his brother, waiting in the dark.

Alex nodded. Slowly. Deliberately.

"Then let's go get him."

John's eyes flickered, just for a second, with something almost like pride.

As night settled heavier outside the windows, father and son sat in the hush of the kitchen, history thick between them.

For the first time in decades, they had a shared mission, and no way back.

Chapter 4: Crossing Lines

The train ride from Manchester to the Polish border felt like a journey into the heart of uncertainty for Alex and his father, John. As they traversed through the European countryside, John's gaze often lingered on the passing scenery, his expression a mix of determination and apprehension. Alex, seated across from him, couldn't help but mirror his father's emotions as the train barrelled forward, the rhythmic clatter of wheels against tracks a constant reminder of their journey's urgency.

When the train finally slowed to a halt at the Polish border, Alex's heart raced with anticipation. Stepping onto the platform, he felt a surge of nervous energy coursing through him, amplified by the sight of uniformed guards patrolling the area. John, however, seemed unfazed as he led Alex towards the border checkpoint, their false passports tucked safely away beneath layers of clothing.

Approaching the border guards, Alex observed their stern expressions and the way they scrutinised each traveller with unwavering focus. His palms grew clammy as they neared the front of the line, his eyes darting nervously between the guards and his father. When it was their turn to present their documents, John's hand remained steady as he handed over their false passports, his demeanour calm and collected despite the tension thick in the air.

As the guards examined their passports, Alex held his breath, every second stretching into an eternity of uncertainty. But to his immense relief, their false identities held up under scrutiny, and after what felt like an eternity, they were waved through the checkpoint and allowed to continue their journey.

Back on another train, Alex couldn't shake the sense of disbelief at the ease with which they had crossed the border. Turning to his father, he couldn't help but voice his astonishment. "How did you manage to get these passports, and why do we need them?"

John's expression softened as he met Alex's gaze, his eyes reflecting a mixture of sadness and resolve. "Sometimes, Alex, the lines between right and wrong become blurred in the pursuit of what's necessary. These passports were provided by contacts I made during my time with UK intelligence. We need them to keep us safe, to protect us from those who would seek to harm us."

As the train rolled on towards Kyiv, Alex mulled over his father's words, the weight of their implications settling heavy in his chest. With each passing mile, the endless landscape outside the window transformed, giving way to sprawling fields and quaint villages that seemed to blur together in a kaleidoscope of colours and shapes.

Finally, as dusk began to settle over the horizon, the train pulled into the bustling station of Kyiv. Stepping onto the platform, Alex was immediately struck by the sights and sounds of the city. The air was alive with the hustle and bustle of people going about their daily lives, their voices blending together in a cacophony of languages and accents.

John led the way through the crowded station, his steps purposeful as he navigated through the throngs of people. Eventually, they emerged onto the bustling streets of Kyiv, they were immediately enveloped in an atmosphere tinged with a sense of both resilience and apprehension. The city, which had been under the shadow of war and the looming threat of Russian aggression for over three years, bore the scars of its tumultuous past with a stoic grace.

Despite the ever-present tension that hung in the air like a heavy fog, there was an undeniable vibrancy to Kyiv, a city that refused to be defined by its struggles. The streets teemed with life, the sounds of laughter and conversation mingling with the steady hum of traffic as people went about their daily lives.

Yet, beneath the surface, there was a palpable undercurrent of fear and uncertainty, a lingering reminder of the conflict that loomed on the horizon. Buildings bore the marks of past battles, their facades pockmarked with holes and shrapnel scars. Graffiti adorned the walls, a testament to the city's resilience in the face of adversity.

Despite the challenges that lay ahead, there was a sense of unity among the people of Kyiv, a shared determination to rebuild and move forward in the wake of destruction. In the chaos and uncertainty, the city remained hopeful, a testament to the indomitable spirit of its inhabitants.

As Alex and John navigated through the crowded streets, they couldn't help but be struck by the juxtaposition of beauty and brutality that defined Kyiv. It was a city that had borne witness to both triumph and tragedy, its streets echoing with the whispers of history and the promise of a better tomorrow.

Their destination was a large nondescript building tucked away in a quiet corner of the city, its windows boarded up and its facade worn with age. As they approached the entrance, Alex couldn't help but feel a sense of trepidation at the thought of what lay beyond its doors.

Stepping inside, Alex and John were immediately greeted by a group of formidable figures, their paramilitary uniforms accentuating their combat-honed physiques. The weight of their Assault rifles seemed to meld seamlessly with their presence, hinting at the countless battles they had weathered. Despite their imposing appearance, there was an unspoken deference in their demeanour as they turned their attention to John.

What caught Alex off guard, however, was the unmistakable air of authority that surrounded his father. In fluent Russian or Ukrainian, John exchanged a few words with the group, his voice barely rising above a whisper amidst the muted din of the surrounding corridor. The revelation left Alex momentarily stunned, his father's commanding presence adding yet another layer of complexity to the enigmatic figure he thought he knew.

As the group conversed, the air crackled with an unspoken tension, their words veiled in secrecy and urgency. Alex strained to catch snippets of their discussion, but the murmur of voices and the distant hum of traffic outside made it impossible to decipher their conversation. The sense of anticipation hung thick in the air, each moment pregnant with the weight of the unknown.

In the adjacent dimly lit room, Alex's eyes were drawn to the stockpile of weapons and military equipment meticulously arranged along the walls. Assault rifles leaned against crates filled with ammunition, while tactical gear and communication devices lay scattered across tables. It was a stark reminder of the dangers that lurked beyond the safety of their sanctuary, a tangible manifestation of the ever-present threat of conflict that loomed over the city of Kyiv like a Specter in the night. And among it all, John stood at the helm, his presence a reassuring anchor in the storm of uncertainty.

Finally, after what felt like an eternity, the men nodded in acknowledgment and led John and Alex deeper into the building. As they disappeared down a dimly lit corridor, Alex couldn't help but wonder what lay in store for him within the confines of his newfound sanctuary. But one thing was certain: whatever awaited him on the other side, they would face it together, father and son, bound by a shared sense of purpose and determination.

As they settled into the safe house, Alex's sense of unease grew palpable as he was instructed to relinquish all his belongings. With anxious agreeing acceptance, he emptied his pockets, watching as his personal effects, his phone, wallet, and keys joined a growing pile on a nearby table. It felt like shedding layers of his identity, leaving behind the trappings of his former life as he prepared to embrace the role thrust upon him.

Next came the directive that struck him with a sense of vulnerability: he was to remove all his clothing. With a mixture of reluctance and resignation, Alex complied, peeling off layer after layer until he stood exposed, stripped down to his barest essence. It was a humbling experience, shedding not just his garments but also the facades he had worn to navigate the world outside.

In exchange for his relinquished attire, Alex was issued new clothing, each item meticulously chosen to obscure his true identity. Gone were the familiar garments that marked him as Alex from Manchester; in their place were nondescript dull green attire that rendered him a stranger even to himself. It was a disconcerting transformation, a reminder of the lengths they were willing to go to ensure their safety in this perilous game of survival.

As he dressed in his new guise, Alex listened intently to the instructions that followed. He was no longer Alex, son of John, but rather an aid worker, a humanitarian on a mission to assist at the frontline of conflict. It was a role he had never imagined himself in, a departure from the life he had known, but one he understood he must embody to navigate the treacherous terrain that lay ahead.

With a deep breath, Alex squared his shoulders and embraced his new identity, steeling himself for the challenges that awaited. As they prepared to depart for the frontline, he couldn't help but feel a surge of apprehension mingled with a flicker of determination. Whatever lay ahead, he was ready to face it head-on, armed not with weapons but with the resilience of the human spirit and the bonds of camaraderie forged in the crucible of adversity. They were going to find Nikolia......

Chapter 5: Dust and Silence

The morning fog had barely lifted when the shelling began again.

Nikolai crouched low in the frozen ditch, his rifle clutched to his chest like a lifeline. Around him, smoke curled through the skeletal remains of birch trees, the once-idyllic countryside now transformed into a churned-up hellscape of cratered fields, collapsed barns, and bloodied snow.

The frontline had once been farmland. Quiet, fertile soil where sunflowers stretched high and old men leaned against fences to smoke. Now it was mud, barbed wire, and broken things, bones, helmets, promises.

A distant thud rolled across the plain. Then another. And another. The ground shook as the artillery drew closer. Always closer.

He could barely hear himself think.

Behind him, someone vomited. Probably Ilya, the boy from Perm who still wore a St. Michael pendant around his neck, even after seeing what the shell had done to the last praying man in their unit.

Next to Nikolai, 19-year-old Misha was trying to light a cigarette with shaking hands. He looked like he'd aged five years in five weeks.

"This isn't what they told us," Misha muttered, voice cracking.

Nikolai didn't answer. What was there to say?

They'd been promised they'd be guarding checkpoints or rebuilding bridges. Humanitarian patrols, they'd said. Stabilisation, not war.

Instead, they were dumped in a frozen trench line near Vuhledar, told to dig and hold until their hands bled. They slept in damp bunkers under collapsed schoolhouses, ate mouldy rations older than they were, and buried the dead in mass graves with stolen shovels.

Some were shot for refusing to advance.

Others simply disappeared, dragged away at night into the forests by shadows who never gave names.

The conscripts joked less now. Laughed even less. Most had stopped counting the days.

"You ever think about home?" Misha asked one night, during a lull.

"Not anymore," Nikolai replied.

He couldn't. Home was abstract now, a memory fading at the edges. He remembered his mother's tea, his brother's laughter, the way his dog used to wait for him by the fence after school.

But even those memories felt like they belonged to someone else.

Later that day, the drone buzzed again.

They'd grown to fear that sound more than the whistle of incoming shells. The buzzing meant eyes. And where there were eyes, there would soon be fire.

Nikolai hugged the dirt.

A second later, the sky turned white.

"There was this explosion," he would say later. "The air got sucked out of my lungs. All I saw was light. It felt like I was pulled underground, like an empty can."

He came to in silence. Not the kind of silence you hear, the kind you feel. No ringing. No shouting. Just dust. Thick and dry in his throat. He blinked through the haze.

Ilya's body was nearby, twisted and charred. The chain around his neck still glinted faintly.

Misha wasn't moving.

The trench had collapsed in parts. The comms wire was severed. The medic, a thin, pale man named Pavel was crying softly as he tied a tourniquet to his own shredded thigh.

Nikolai forced himself upright. His left ear was bleeding. His rifle was gone.

He limped toward the crater, half-crawling.

Everywhere around him, bodies not just dead, but torn apart. Unrecognisable.

He knelt beside Misha.

Still breathing. Barely.

That night, Nikolai didn't speak. He sat beside the wreckage of a troop carrier, wrapped in a damp blanket, his boots still soaked in blood and slush.

He watched the sky. Not for enemy aircraft, for stars.

But they were gone. Hidden behind black smoke and the endless orange of burning fields.

And yet, somewhere beneath the terror, beneath the numbness and grief, something inside him refused to break.

Not yet.

Maybe it was instinct. Maybe it was the tiny voice inside that told him this wasn't all there was. That something, someone, still waited beyond this horror.

Across the field, the night lit up again. Another town shelled. Another house gone.

And Nikolai, son of a father he never truly knew, whispered his brother's name into the darkness.

"Alex..."

Then the fire resumed.

And the silence was shattered once more.

Chapter 6: Into the Grey

As John and Alex prepared to leave the relative safety of the Kyiv safe house, a palpable tension hung in the air, thick as the bitter winter chill that gripped the city. With a small contingent of Ukrainian soldiers at their side, they made their way through the dimly lit corridors, the flickering glow of overhead lights casting long shadows that danced along the walls.

"Stay close, Alex," John's voice was low but firm, his hand resting reassuringly on his son's shoulder as they navigated the maze-like corridors of the safe house.

Emerging into the frigid night air, they were met with the sight of two tatty looking 4x4 Toyota vehicles waiting patiently at the curb. The vehicles, battered and worn from years of use, seemed to blend seamlessly into the urban landscape, their faded exteriors bearing the scars of countless journeys into the heart of conflict.

"Looks like we're taking the scenic route," John remarked dryly, a hint of wry humour in his voice as he gestured towards the vehicles.

As they climbed into the cramped confines of the vehicles, Alex couldn't shake the sense of foreboding that settled over him like a heavy blanket. The air inside the vehicle was thick with tension, the silence punctuated only by the low hum of the engine and the occasional crackle of static from the radio.

"Alex," John said, his voice cutting through the hum of the engine like a field order. "What we're walking into isn't just dangerous, it's unpredictable. No hesitation. No second-guessing. We do this clean. Stay sharp. Follow my lead. If things go sideways, you move."

Alex turned, his expression hardening into something colder, more focused, the switch flipping. The civvie exterior peeled away, replaced by the steel-eyed calm of someone who'd once lived on the edge.

"I've got it," he said, quiet but resolute. "You don't need to worry about me."

John gave a subtle nod, though a flicker of something, regret, maybe, passed across his face. "If I go down out there," he added, "you get yourself and Nikolai out. There's a go-bag at the safe house, new IDs, fallback routes, cash. Use it. Burn everything else."

Alex didn't flinch. "I won't need it. But if I do, I'll get us home."

Alex's Jaw tightened as he swallowed hard, the weight of his father's words settling heavy in his chest. With a nod of affirmation, John turned his attention back to the road ahead, his grip on the steering wheel tightening as they continued their journey into the heart of the unknown. In the darkness of the night, with the spectre of war looming large on the horizon, father and son shared a silent vow to see each other through to the end, no matter what challenges lay ahead.

They made their way through the city streets, where they encountered a series of military security checkpoints, their progress slowed by the meticulous scrutiny of armed guards. Each checkpoint served as a stark reminder of the ever-present danger that lurked just beyond the city limits, a reminder that they were entering into a world where the rules of engagement were dictated by the whims of war.

On the outskirts, the city was cloaked in darkness, the only illumination coming from the random flickering streetlights that lined the deserted streets. The cold winter weather seemed to seep into their bones, a constant reminder of the harsh realities of life on the frontline.

"Are you sure we're doing the right thing, Dad?" Alex's voice was barely above a whisper, the weight of uncertainty evident in his words as he glanced nervously out the window at the desolate streets passing by.

"We don't have a choice, Alex," John replied, his tone grave but resolute. "Nikolai needs our help, and we're the only ones who can give it to him."

Finally, as they left the city behind and ventured out into the vast countryside, a sense of unease settled over the group like a heavy fog. The landscape stretched out before them, a desolate expanse of open fields and barren landscape of the Steppe that seemed to stretch on for miles.

They continued their journey towards Avdiivka, where John had last heard from Nikolai, Alex couldn't help but feel a knot of fear tightening in his chest. But with his father by his side and the unwavering determination of their Ukrainian allies, he knew that they would stop at nothing to find Nikolai and bring him home, no matter the cost.

As they navigated the unforgiving terrain of the war-torn landscape, Alex couldn't help but marvel at the transformation he had witnessed in his father, John. Gone was the unassuming man he thought he knew, replaced instead by a shadowy enigma who seemed to thrive amidst the chaos and uncertainty of the operational war zone.

In this environment, John exuded a quiet confidence, his every movement calculated and deliberate as he led their small unit into the danger ahead. To most, he appeared to be nothing more than an average, understated individual, blending seamlessly into the background like a chameleon in the shadows. But to Alex, who now saw his father through a different lens, he was a revelation, a man shrouded in mystery and intrigue.

There was a darkness to John, an unknown side that Alex had never before glimpsed. In the heat of this tense environment, he was a force to be reckoned with, his instincts honed by years of experience in the clandestine world of intelligence. His eyes, once warm and familiar, now held a steely resolve, betraying none of the emotions that churned beneath the surface.

As they pressed forward, navigating the treacherous terrain with a sense of urgency, Alex couldn't shake the feeling of unease that gnawed at him. He had always known that his father was involved in activities that lay beyond the realm of ordinary life, but witnessing firsthand the depths to which he would go to achieve his objectives was a sobering realisation.

As their two-vehicle convoy closed in on the outskirts of Avdiivka, the landscape underwent a chilling metamorphosis, transforming from the serene countryside into a war-torn nightmare. Burnt-out rusting vehicles littered the roadside like twisted metal carcasses, their skeletal frames a grim testament to the ferocity of the fighting that had ravaged the area. Homes and buildings lay in ruins, their shattered windows and crumbling facades silent witnesses to the devastation that had befallen them.

The scenes that lay before them were a harrowing tableau of destruction and despair. Damaged trees stood as sentinels of the destruction, their gnarled branches reaching out like accusing fingers towards the heavens. Dead animals littered the roadside, their lifeless bodies serving as grim reminders of the toll that war had exacted on both man and beast.

As they pressed forward, the stench of decay hung heavy in the air, a sickening miasma that permeated every breath they took. Decomposing bodies lay at the roadside, their vacant stares frozen in silent agony as they bore witness to the horrors of war. It was a sight that turned the stomach and chilled the soul, a stark reminder of the human cost of the conflict that raged on unabated.

Evidence of very serious fighting was everywhere; the scars of battle etched deep into the very fabric of the land. Pockmarked craters marred the earth, the remnants of explosions that had torn through the ground like a wrathful deity unleashed. Shell casings littered the ground like discarded confetti; their glinting surfaces a macabre reminder of the relentless violence that had consumed the area.

John and Alex were keenly aware of the dangers that surrounded them on all sides. In this desolate landscape, death lurked around every corner, its cold embrace waiting to claim those who dared to tread its unforgiving path. Yet, despite the overwhelming despair that threatened to engulf them, they pressed on, driven by a singular purpose.

As they reached the small village a few kilometres from Avdiivka, they were met by other soldiers at a checkpoint, their war-weary faces etched with the exhaustion of endless conflict. Among them stood the leader, a man named Danylo, whom John greeted with a firm handshake and a nod of recognition.

"Danylo," John's voice carried a note of respect, "it's good to see you again, though I wish it were under better circumstances."

Danylo returned the gesture with a weary smile, his voice rough with fatigue. "Likewise, John. But in times like these, I'm grateful for every familiar face I can find."

Their exchange was brief, but in the shared glance between them, there was an unspoken understanding of the trials they faced together on the frontline. With a silent nod of affirmation, they prepared to face the challenges ahead.

Danylo, a man whose very name meant "God is my Judge," had once been a humble garage apprentice before the specter of war descended upon his homeland. In a courageous act of patriotism, he traded in his wrenches for weapons, joining the ranks of those who stood ready to defend their country against tyranny. His hands, once calloused from years of honest labour beneath the bonnets of cars, now bore the unmistakable scars of battle, a testament to the sacrifices made in the pursuit of freedom.

Danylo was the kind of man who commands a room without saying a word. Tall, broad-shouldered, and battle-hardened, his presence is both inspiring and intimidating. His face tells a story lined not by age, but by war, loss, and resolve. A scar runs from his left temple to the edge of his jaw, a silent reminder of the price he's paid for freedom.

Born in a small town near Lviv, Danylo joined the military young for his national service, rising quickly through the ranks due to his tactical mind, calmness under fire, and unbreakable loyalty to his comrades. He left official service with honour, but when war returned to his homeland, so did Danylo this time as a unit commander in the heart of occupied territory.

Danylo is not just a fighter he's a leader. His men would follow him into hell, and some have. He leads from the front, eats last, sleeps least, and carries the weight of every casualty. Though stern and often silent, those close to him know he carries a deep well of compassion, especially for civilians caught in the crossfire. He despises cruelty and values discipline, loyalty, and justice.

In battle, he is a strategist and a warrior. In peace, he is a ghost always moving, never safe, always watching. Despite the chaos around him, Danylo holds onto hope: not naive optimism, but the kind forged in blood and belief. He fights not just for victory, but for the soul of his country.

John maneuvered his Toyota through the narrow streets until they reached a set of nondescript buildings on the outskirts of this small village. A barn door creaked open, and they drove inside, the echo of their engines fading into the quiet darkness as they switched them off. The threat from Russian artillery and drones loomed large overhead, and they couldn't afford to linger out in the open any longer than necessary.

Once out of the vehicles, Alex was introduced to Danylo and his fellow soldiers. Their faces were weathered by the harsh realities of life on the frontline, their uniforms bearing the stains of sweat and blood. Despite their weariness, there was a sense of quiet determination among them, a shared resolve to defend their homeland at all costs.

Danylo briefed John on the current situation in the area, detailing the latest movements of Russian forces and the ongoing struggles faced by the Ukrainian defenders. His voice was tinged with weariness, but beneath the fatigue, there burned a fierce determination to see his country through to victory.

It was agreed that later that night, under the cover of darkness, John would attempt to make contact with Nikolai on the other side of the front line. The Ukrainians were eager to help, hoping to glean valuable intelligence about the Russian fighting capability in the area from Nikolai's firsthand accounts.

As the night fell and the shadows lengthened, John couldn't shake the sense of urgency that gripped him like a vice. The fate of his son hung in the balance, and every moment wasted was a moment lost in their race against time.

Alex stood shoulder to shoulder with the men, their breath fogging in the cold air. Their expressions were carved by war itself, uniforms frayed and dust-caked, eyes hollowed by sleepless nights and the heavy silence of fallen brothers. Around him, the barn was dimly lit, quiet except for the occasional creak of timber and the dull, distant echo of artillery. The air was heavy with smoke, diesel, and something else, expectation.

But he wasn't some helpless observer thrown into their world.

He knew the cadence of war. He'd lived it.

The worn concrete beneath his boots, the smell of old blood and wet soil, the way a soldier shifts his weight before reaching for his weapon, none of it was unfamiliar. It was muscle memory now, buried but intact. The years between his final deployment and today had been full of self-destruction and rebuilding, but beneath it all, Alex Winters was still a soldier. A predator taught to survive in chaos.

He glanced around at the Ukrainian fighters, eyes sunken, jaws tight. Men who had seen too much and yet still stood ready. Their silence wasn't awkward; it was trained. Calculated. They assessed him as one of their own might assess a new arrival. Not for weakness, but for steadiness. And he gave them nothing to doubt.

Still, a flicker of hesitation sparked inside him, not fear, exactly, but an echo of self-doubt. A shadow that whispered *You've been out too long. They've bled for this place. You haven't.* For a second, the weight of that truth pressed into his chest like a boot.

But then he exhaled. Slow. Measured. And the doubt began to fade.

He wasn't here to play hero. He was here because of blood, his father's, and a half-brother he'd never known. And because no one else was coming to get the job done.

His gaze shifted to his father, who stood conferring with Danylo like it was just another op. And maybe it was. To John Winters, this chaos was just a return to familiar ground. But for Alex, it was something more. A test, not just of skill, but of purpose.

He adjusted the weight of his gear, the straps biting into his shoulders in a way that felt almost reassuring. His breathing steadied. His vision sharpened. The world outside the barn fell away until there was only the mission, the team, the terrain.

Whatever lay ahead, gunfire, betrayal, blood, he wouldn't flinch.

He didn't need to be one of them.

He just needed to remember who he was.

Suddenly Artillery shells began to rain down nearby, the thunderous explosions sucking the air from the barn and sending shockwaves reverberating through the building, reality crashed back upon Alex with frightening force. While the war-weary soldiers remained steadfast, their faces weathered but resolute, Alex couldn't stifle the instinctual flinch that seized his body. The shelling, though not directly threatening, was terrifyingly close for Alex's comfort.

Each explosion echoed like a sinister drumbeat, punctuating the air with the sharp scent of smoke and the acrid taste of fear. While the seasoned soldiers seemed unperturbed, Alex couldn't shake the creeping sense of dread that coiled in the pit of his stomach. It was a stark reminder of the fragility of life in this unforgiving battleground, where danger lurked in every shadow and survival was never assured.

As the bombardment continued, the barn walls quivered with each concussive blast, the ground trembling beneath their feet. Despite the cacophony of chaos outside, a heavy silence fell over the room, broken only by the ragged breaths of those within.

In the face of such sudden and overwhelming danger, Alex knew he had to steel himself against his own fear. With every nerve on edge and every heartbeat thundering in his ears, he stood resolute, determined to weather the storm alongside his comrades. For in the crucible of conflict, it was only by confronting the fears head-on that he could hope to emerge victorious. Alex braced himself for the trials that lay ahead.

Chapter 7: Ghosts in the Sky

Later that night Alex entered a bunker adjacent to the barn while his father was arranging some hot food and was met with a scene that seemed surreal in the chaos of war. Three young men, clad in scruffy military uniforms, sat huddled around a makeshift gaming console, their faces illuminated by the soft glow of the screen. At first glance, they appeared no different from a group of friends gathered round at a mate's house, lost in the immersive world of a video game.

But as Alex drew closer, he realised with a jolt that their reality was far removed from the virtual world of shoot 'em up games. These young men were drone operators, their PlayStation-like handsets not controllers for a game, but tools of war used to strike real, living targets several kilometres away on the front line.

Their conversation was punctuated by bursts of static and terse commands; spoken in a language Alex couldn't understand but that crackled with tension. He could sense the weight of their responsibility, the gravity of their mission pressing down on them like a dead weight.

He watched in awe when one of the young men shouted out in celebration, his voice tinged with triumph. Though Alex couldn't comprehend the words, he could feel the tension in the air, the electric anticipation as they awaited confirmation of their strike.

When their target seemed to be hit, they erupted in cheers and high-fives, their jubilant shouts echoing off the bunker walls. It was a surreal moment, a stark reminder of the disconnect between the virtual world they inhabited and the harsh realities of war on the other side of their front line. There was no sympathy towards the enemy.

In that moment, Alex gained a newfound respect for the sacrifices made by those who fought on the front lines, both seen and unseen. For these young drone operators, their war was waged not with guns and grenades, but with pixels and precision strikes, a silent and deadly dance in the skies above. And as the distant echoes of explosions reverberated through the air, he knew that their struggle was far from over, their fate bound to the whims of war for as long as the conflict raged on. As Alex observed the drone operators in the bunker, a shiver ran down his spine, his thoughts consumed by the very real threat posed by these unmanned aerial vehicles. In recent months, their use had skyrocketed, with both sides in the conflict employing drones to devastating effect. The skies had become a battleground in their own right, and anyone moving in the open risked becoming a target.

The thought of traversing the open terrain towards the front lines filled Alex with a sense of dread. With drones patrolling the skies above, every step taken was fraught with danger, every moment spent exposed a gamble with life and limb. The constant buzz of electric motors overhead served as a chilling reminder of the ever-present threat lurking just beyond the ability to see.

In the face of such peril, Alex couldn't help but feel a creeping sense of vulnerability. Unlike the soldiers around him, who had grown accustomed to the constant spectre of death, he was ill-prepared for the dangers that awaited him on the frontline. His heart raced at the mere thought of being targeted by one of those deadly machines, his mind conjuring vivid images of the devastation they could wreak.

Yet, despite his fear, Alex knew that he had to press on. Nikolai's fate hung in the balance, and he couldn't afford to let his own apprehensions stand in the way of their mission. With a silent prayer for protection, he steeled himself for the journey ahead, his determination burning bright in the face of adversity. For in the crucible of war, it was only by confronting their fears head-on that they could hope to emerge victorious.

In the dimly lit bunker, John huddled over his secure phone, his brow furrowed in concentration as he spoke in hushed tones to his son, Nikolai, on the other side of the front line.

"Nikolai, listen carefully," John's voice was steady, reassuring. "We've arranged for your surrender, but we need to be cautious. The signal will be a green flare near the church in Berdychiv at 0200hrs on Saturday Morning. When you see it, you must run towards it, dropping your rifle and raising your hands to show you're not a threat to the Ukrainian troops."

Nikolai's voice crackled over the line, tense with anxiety. "I understand. But I'm worried about being overheard by my patrol leaders. They're suspicious of anyone."

John's heart clenched at the desperation in his son's tone. "Stay strong, Nikolai. We've planned for every contingency. Look for a burnt-out truck near the church as an additional marker and head to its right. We'll be waiting on our side of the trenches to guide you to safety."

As the call ended, John couldn't shake the swell of fear that gripped him. The thought of his son navigating the perilous landscape behind enemy lines filled him with a sense of urgency, propelling him to action.

With a silent moment of reflection for their safety, John and Alex prepared to make their way to Berdychiv, where Nikolai's fate hung in the balance. For in the crucible of war, family was the strongest bond of all, and they would stop at nothing to ensure Nikolai's safe return.

Chapter 8: The Rescue

Under the moonlit shadows of the ancient church in Berdychiv, Alex and John moved silently through the trench lines, the cold glow of stars above offering little comfort. The ground sucked at their boots, thick with mud and war debris, while the cold dry air buzzed with tension. Somewhere ahead, beneath layers of barbed wire and darkness, Nikolai waited.

They were close now.

Ukrainian fighters, led by the unflinching Danylo, guided them forward with short gestures and sharper eyes. Their rifles were ready. Every man knew the mission. Every man knew the risk.

Alex stole a glance at his father.

John Winters was calm. Focused. But beneath the calm was something else a hard glint in his eyes, something deeper than duty. This wasn't just an operation. This was personal.

They reached a shell-cratered position on the edge of no man's land. The signal was moments away.

Then, the flare.

It hissed into the sky like a demon's cry, bursting green across the battlefield. Harsh shadows snapped into view. The ground turned silver and black.

On the far side, Nikolai moved.

He bolted from cover with the desperation of someone who knew there might be no second chance. Gunfire erupted immediately. Shouts in Russian. Muzzle flashes flared from the treeline.

"Contact!" Danylo barked. "Cover fire, now!"

Alex fired blindly into the dark as Nikolai sprinted, zigzagging across the churned soil. A round clipped the dirt near his foot. Another grazed his sleeve. He stumbled, then pushed harder.

Through the smoke, John moved.

Without hesitation, he vaulted the trench and ran toward his son. The battlefield swallowed him whole.

"Dad!" Alex shouted into his comms.

"I've got him!" came John's voice, tight and breathless.

Seconds later, John's arm wrapped around Nikolai and hauled him to cover behind a fallen stone wall. Blood ran from Nikolai's arm, but he was alive. Dazed, but alive.

Alex reached them, his rifle low, scanning for threats.

"You're insane," he muttered to John, half in awe.

John gave a tired, crooked smile. "Maybe. But I got him."

Danylo's men moved quickly, laying suppressive fire as the small group pulled back into the Ukrainian trench network. By the time they ducked behind the sandbags near the old church, the immediate danger had passed.

Nikolai sat slumped, blinking slowly, mumbling in Russian. John knelt beside him, checking his pulse. Alive but clearly malnourished from weeks in the trenches.

And for a moment, just a moment, there was a breath of relief.

"Medic!" Alex shouted over his shoulder. "We need a medic here!"

Then it happened.

From the edge of the trench, where the shadows met the moonlight, a figure emerged. Unrecognised. Hooded. Calm.

Before anyone could react, he raised a suppressed pistol and fired once.

Thwip.

The shot hit John squarely in the chest, dead centre.

John gasped, staggered, and collapsed backward against the trench wall. The medic who had just arrived froze in shock. Chaos erupted again.

Alex turned, raised his weapon, but the figure was already moving, vanishing into the smoke, slipping between soldiers like a phantom. A second shot cracked the air, hitting no one, and then he was gone.

Gone.

"Sniper?" Danylo shouted.

"No," Alex said, dropping to his knees beside his father. "That was up close."

John's eyes flicked open, just for a second. His gaze found Alex, then Nikolai. There was something in his expression. Pride. Sadness. Peace.

He tried to speak.

No sound came.

His hand went limp.

Alex pressed his palm to his father's chest, but the blood soaked through too quickly. Too much. Too deep.

John Winters was gone.

The man who had survived wars, betrayal, and secrets had been silenced, not on the battlefield, but in supposed safety. Executed.

Gunfire erupted down the line as Ukrainian soldiers tried to chase the shooter. But whoever he was, he had vanished.

Alex stared at the trail of blood on his hands.

Danylo stepped beside him, grim. "It wasn't random," he said. "That was a message."

Alex nodded, jaw tight. "He got Nikolai out. He did what he came to do."

Nikolai groaned, lifting his head slowly. He saw John's body, and for the first time, his expression cracked, pain flashing through his bloodied face.

Alex leaned closer to his half-brother.

"We're not leaving him here," he said.

Nikolai gave the faintest nod.

Together, they would get John home.

But first, they would find out who killed him and why.

Chapter 9: Brothers in Ashes

The cramped cellar stank of diesel and damp earth. A single bulb flickered above them, casting long shadows over the shape beneath the tarp.

John Winters lay still wrapped in a military-issue poncho, blood dried into the fabric. His face was covered, but both sons could picture him perfectly: the unreadable expression, the tired eyes that never missed a thing. Now, finally silent.

Finally, Danylo spoke.

"I'm sorry," he said, quietly. "Your father… he was a good man. One of the best I ever knew."

Alex nodded numbly, staring into the dark.

He couldn't speak.

Not yet.

Not until he knew the secrets he never got to finish revealing.

Alex stared at the body for a long time. Nikolai sat across the room, arms crossed, gaze fixed on nothing.

They hadn't spoken much since the firefight.

When they did, it went badly.

"I suppose you think you knew him," Nikolai said in broken English. "You didn't."

Alex glanced up. "And you did?"

"I *lived* with him," Nikolai snapped. "You had him on your shelf, picture frame, probably next to your bloody graduation."

Alex took a step forward. "Don't pretend you knew the man. He abandoned us both."

Silence followed. Heavy. Uncomfortable. True.

Alex turned away. He didn't want to fight. Not here. Not in front of *him*.

"We need to get him home," Alex said finally. "To England."

Nikolai looked up. "Why? He wasn't English to me."

"Because he deserves that. Because he risked everything coming here for you."

Nikolai stood. His face, angular and scarred, softened just a fraction. "Then we do it. But your country won't want us back with the truth. And mine wants us dead."

Alex nodded. "That's why we do it like he would've."

They met the contact at dawn.

A woman named Ivana, in her fifties, eyes as sharp as John's had ever been. She had worked with him once in Bucharest, years ago. Old favours still carried weight.

"Your father was many things," she said, handing them a bundle of documents. "But above all, prepared."

Inside the envelope: two sets of EU passports, with forged visas and medical transport credentials. Names: *Adam Clarke* and *Nikolai Petrovich*. The third passport was John's under a diplomatic alias.

"Travel by night," she warned. "Avoid checkpoints. The eastern roads are crawling with militia and worse. This," she said, pulling out a folded document, "is your route. Stay away from Khmelnytskyi. Too much Russian surveillance."

"What about Polish border patrols?" Nikolai asked.

Ivana smiled grimly. "You leave the talking to me."

The journey began in silence.

They rode in the back of a decrepit ambulance, posing as medical volunteers transporting a body for burial. The roads were rough, cratered by shelling, patrolled by jumpy soldiers with too many questions and too little trust.

At one checkpoint, a young Ukrainian soldier raised his rifle as they slowed.

"Papers!" he barked.

Alex's hands didn't shake but only just. He passed the documents forward. The soldier examined them in the beam of a headlamp. Too long. Too quiet.

Then, a nod.

"Slava Ukraini," the soldier said, stepping back.

"Heroyam slava," Nikolai replied quietly.

They moved on.

That night, under the cover of a ruined barn, they shared a flask and lit a small fire out of sight from the road.

Nikolai finally spoke. "He used to whistle when he cooked. Same tune. Over and over."

Alex stared at the flames. "He used to sit in his study with the door closed for hours. I thought he was writing. Maybe he was just hiding."

Nikolai looked at him, eyebrows lifted. "From what?"

Alex took a breath. "From everything he did. Everything he was."

They didn't say anything after that. But the silence was different this time, no longer combative, just... shared.

A brittle kind of understanding began to form. A thin bridge built on the only thing they both had left.

By the time they crossed the border into Poland, the ambulance was falling apart, and so were they physically, emotionally. But John's body was still with them, and their resolve had only hardened.

As they pulled into the Polish border facility near Rzeszów.

Alex looked over at his half-brother.

"You still think we didn't know him?"

Nikolai hesitated. Then: "No. I think... maybe we only knew pieces. He gave us different parts of himself."

Alex nodded. "Then maybe it's time we figure out who he really was."

And in the pocket of his coat, the Microdrive they'd recovered from John's shoe seemed heavier now.

Waiting.

Chapter 10: The Militia's Refusal

The room smelled of disinfectant and damp wool. A weak strip of light leaked through a frosted window, illuminating a metal table. On it sat a single folder thin, dog-eared marked WINTERS, JOHN ***** HOLD FOR VERIFICATION *****.

Alex stood tense by the door, jaw tight, while Nikolai paced slowly, arms folded across his chest. Two border officials in olive uniforms stood at the far end, flanked by an officer from the Polish Internal Security - Agencja Bezpieczeństwa Wewnętrznego, watching them both with unreadable expressions.

"We've come a long way," Alex said, his voice strained, "risked our lives, all we're asking is for my father's body to be released. He deserves a proper final resting place. In England."

The lead official, a grizzled man in his sixties with nicotine-stained fingers, raised his eyes to meet Alex's.

"That's not your father anymore," he said coldly. "That's a political complication."

Alex took a step forward. "He was *British*. A retired operative. He died trying to rescue his son."

"Yes," the officer replied evenly, "and possibly while passing information to both sides."

Alex froze. "What?"

The official tapped the folder. "Multiple IDs. Contradictory records in our systems. Messages intercepted between Ukrainian and Russian operatives with reference to someone matching his description. Your father didn't just cross borders, he crossed lines."

Nikolai suddenly stiffened. "Let me see that file."

The official narrowed his eyes. "You don't have clearance."

Nikolai stepped forward, voice sharp. "He was my father too. You think he worked both sides? Then you didn't know him."

"Did *you*?" the officer shot back. "Because from where we're standing, we see a man with deep ties to British intelligence, operating under multiple aliases in a live warzone, contacting both Ukrainian and Russian assets. He didn't just wander into this. He was part of something far more complex."

Nikolai glanced at Alex, then turned away, jaw clenched. His voice lowered. "He told me once... people think spies are loyal. But they're not. Not really. They're useful. Until they're not."

Alex frowned. "You think it's true?"

Nikolai didn't answer.

The silence stretched.

Outside, the wind cut through their jackets as they stepped out of the grey government building. The world was muted, the buzz of a nearby checkpoint, the hum of distant traffic, but to Alex, it felt like everything had shifted.

"We have to get him back," he muttered. "No matter what they believe."

"They won't release him," Nikolai said. "Not without proof he wasn't playing both sides. And if he was..."

Alex turned, angry. "*You're seriously entertaining that? He died saving you.*"

Nikolai didn't flinch. "I know. But that doesn't mean he didn't carry secrets they don't want exposed. The timing, his presence here, the data on that drive... he wasn't just looking for me. He was *doing something.*"

Alex exhaled slowly, forcing calm.

"Then we find out what it was. We clear his name. We finish what he started."

Nikolai raised an eyebrow. "And if what he started was... something darker?"

Alex's eyes didn't waver. "Then we bring it into the light."

They stood in silence for a moment, two brothers bound now by blood, grief, and a father they never truly knew.

Then Nikolai pulled something from inside his coat, a battered key, old and brass, with an inscription along the side in Cyrillic.

Alex took it, turning it over. "Where did this come from?"

"He gave it to me. In case things went wrong."

Alex looked up. "What's it for?"

Nikolai's voice was low. "A lockbox. Hidden in a safehouse. Kyiv."

Alex stared at him. "You're saying we go back?"

Nikolai nodded. "If we want answers, it's where they'll be."

Alex looked toward the horizon east, toward the smoke, toward the place they'd just escaped.

The silence was his answer.

They were going back in.

Chapter 11: Extraction Plan

The train station in Rzeszów bustled with exhausted families, foreign aid workers, and grim-faced soldiers in transit. Alex and Nikolai sat apart on a bench near the far end of the platform, their eyes scanning the crowd, their shoulders hunched against the cold.

In Nikolai's hand was the key, the old brass one with the Cyrillic etching rolling slowly between his fingers like a coin of fate.

"This is madness," Alex muttered, eyes fixed on the timetables overhead. "We just got out of Ukraine alive. Now we're going *back in*?"

Nikolai didn't look up. "Dad didn't die for us to walk away. That key leads to a safehouse. If there's anything that can prove who he really was or what he was doing it'll be there."

Alex ran a hand through his hair. "And if it proves he *was* working both sides?"

"Then we learn *why*," Nikolai said flatly. "And what he was trying to stop."

Back at the safe flat in the outskirts, the lights were dimmed, blinds drawn. The air was thick with tension and cigarette smoke, Danylo stood at the small kitchen counter, staring at a map of Kyiv and sipping coffee like it was ammunition.

"You realise," he said without turning, "if you go back, you're no longer observers. You're targets."

"We already are," Nikolai replied. "Polish security flagged us. The British won't intervene without plausible deniability. The Russians probably think I'm dead."

Alex leaned forward, pointing at the map. "This area here Podil. He took me there when I was a kid. Said it was a ghost from his past. Could that be where the safehouse is?"

Danylo circled the district with a pencil. "It's possible. A lot of Cold War-era drop points and safehouses in that part of the city. Some of them still 'unofficially' active."

He looked up at Alex. "You'll need forged papers, clean comms, and someone who can get you in without alerting border surveillance."

Alex nodded. "Can you get us that?"

Danylo exhaled. "I can get you *most* of it. But once you cross the line, you're on your own. The city's crawling with surveillance, Russian agents, Ukrainian counterintelligence, mercenaries... And the worst of them aren't wearing uniforms."

Nikolai cracked a faint smile. "Good. That means we won't stand out."

Danylo didn't smile back. "This isn't a game."

"No," Nikolai said, eyes steely. "It's our father's truth. And someone killed him to keep it buried."

That night, the brothers prepared.

Nikolai disassembled and cleaned the pistol Danylo had given him, laying it carefully into a false-bottom bag. Alex sat at the small desk, translating the markings on the brass key using a Ukrainian phrasebook and the few Russian words John had taught him as a boy.

"*Shkaf-35... Kryvyi Rih vault system... Level three access*," he muttered. "This wasn't just a flat. This was part of something bigger."

Nikolai looked over. "You think John was planning something?"

"I think he was finishing something."

The next morning, just before dawn, they stood at the border crossing in Lublin, still dressed as aid workers. Danylo handed Alex a sealed envelope.

"What's this?" Alex asked.

"In case you don't make it back. It has coordinates to a contact in Warsaw who can help get John's body back... if you can't."

Alex met his eyes. "We'll make it."

Danylo gave a slow nod. "I know. But understand this, if what's in that safehouse is as dangerous as I think, you're going to have enemies in more than one country."

He looked between them. "Don't just think like sons. Think like soldiers."

Alex and Nikolai exchanged a glance.

For the first time, there was no tension between them, just resolve.

As they stepped onto the bus bound for the Ukrainian border, the landscape rolled past like a fading memory. Fields. Villages.

The border came into view: barbed wire, sandbags, and checkpoints.

Alex gripped the edge of his seat.

"Nikolai," he said quietly, "whatever's in that safehouse... you sure you want to know?"

Nikolai stared ahead, his voice low.

"No. But I need to."

Chapter 12: The Safehouse in Podil

Kyiv was still a city holding its breath.

The brothers moved through it like shadows, disguised as aid couriers, their papers loose enough to pass quick inspections but not convincing enough for close scrutiny. The streets of Podil were quiet but watchful. Tired eyes stared from shuttered windows. Drone buzzes and distant mortar echoes marked the tempo of the city's new rhythm.

By late afternoon, they reached the building.

It was a five-storey tenement half-sunk into the street, its pale-yellow plaster cracked like old bone. On the doorframe, faded Cyrillic numbers matched the inscription on the brass key: Шкаф-35.

"This is it," Nikolai said under his breath.

Alex hesitated at the threshold, sensing the ghosts that lingered here. His father had walked through this door, maybe years ago, maybe recently. Maybe more than once.

The hallway inside was dark and smelled of mildew and dust. The stairs groaned beneath their boots as they climbed to the third floor.

At the end of the corridor: a grey steel door, unmarked, locked.

Nikolai stepped forward, inserted the key, and turned it with a soft click.

The door swung inward.

The safehouse was a single room, bare, concrete walls, no windows. But it was cleaner than expected. Organised. Lived in.

A desk against the far wall. A metal filing cabinet. A bed in the corner. And near the ceiling, a vented panel likely masking a backup air filtration system the kind used during chemical alert protocols.

Alex stepped inside slowly. The door closed behind them with a quiet metallic thud.

"Jesus," he whispered. "It's like time stopped in here."

Nikolai moved to the desk. There were maps of eastern Europe, dog-eared passports, notepads filled with codes, phone numbers, and grid coordinates.

He opened the top drawer, inside, wrapped in oilskin, was a sealed envelope. On the front, in John's careful handwriting:

If you are reading this, I'm already dead.

Alex and Nikolai stood over the desk as Nikolai slit the envelope open.

Inside: a letter, a photograph, and a flash drive.

Alex picked up the photo first.

It was old, maybe 1980s grainy, taken with a long lens. It showed three men standing on a balcony in Moscow, mid-conversation. One of them was clearly John.

The second man was Russian a former GRU officer Nikolai recognised but couldn't name.

The third was the shock.

"Is that... British?" Alex asked.

Nikolai nodded slowly. "MI6."

"What the hell was Dad doing meeting with *both* of them?"

Nikolai unfolded the letter and began to read aloud:
"To my sons —

If you've made it here, you already know I've failed to finish what I started. I never expected to survive this. I never expected to bring both of you together under these circumstances. But if you're reading this, the choice is no longer mine, it's yours.

What I uncovered during my final operations wasn't just rogue intelligence. It was something older. A Cold War alliance that never dissolved, a black directive between elements of MI6, GRU, and

NATO-*linked corporations.*

They've kept wars going for profit. Proxy conflicts, false-flag operations, destabilisations masked as liberation. And now, they've set their eyes on Ukraine as their next permanent war theatre. I had proof, I still do.

But I couldn't act without exposing people I once trusted. People I trained with. People I killed beside.

The flash drive contains what I managed to extract before they found me. Names. Routes. Weapon shipments. Accounts. A project called Helix; if you've heard of it, you already know how far this goes. The decision is yours: bury it… or burn them all with it.

— J.W."

Silence fell like ash.

Nikolai looked at the flash drive, then back at the letter.

"Helix," he said slowly. "I've heard whispers. Rumours. An old operation supposedly dismantled after the Soviet collapse. But some say it just went dark. Changed hands."

Alex stepped back, stunned. "So, Dad wasn't just rescuing you. He was trying to stop a war… before it starts again."

"No," Nikolai corrected him. "He was trying to stop the *same war*, the one that never really ended."

They searched the safehouse for more. In the false bottom of the filing cabinet, they found photos of arms shipments arriving at nondescript airfields. One of the locations was marked in pen: Wyton, UK a base Alex recognised from his childhood, supposedly decommissioned.

Another document listed encrypted bank transfers vast sums moving through shell companies registered in Singapore, Geneva, and Istanbul.

And in a final drawer, they found another sealed envelope.

On it, just two words:

Kestrel Protocol.

Alex's hand shook slightly as he held it.

Nikolai's voice was low. "You ready for this?"

"No," Alex said. "But we're past ready now."

John Winters had been many things, a father, a spy, a ghost in a war that never ended.

But now, his truth had become *their* mission.

And the deeper they went, the more dangerous it would become.

Chapter 13: The Cryptic Code

Kyiv pulsed with quiet dread.

By day, checkpoints and roadblocks broke up the flow of traffic and a sense of normality filled a city surrounded by war. But by night, the city breathed in whispers, shadows moving between crumbling apartment blocks, lights flickering in basements where resistance plans were discussed, and plans drawn up. The occasional explosion could be heard in the distance as Russian drones found their targets.

Nikolai sat hunched over a battered laptop on a makeshift table, his face lit by the pale blue glow of the screen. Alex paced behind him, his nerves fraying with each passing hour.

"You sure you can break it?" Alex asked, nodding to the Microdrive plugged into the machine.

"It's not about breaking it," Nikolai replied, fingers flying across the keyboard. "It's about remembering the pattern."

He paused. "He taught it to me when I was a kid. Said it was a game. A way to keep secrets locked away inside your own head."

He typed a single phrase into the prompt line.

Truth is the last safehouse.

A moment passed.

The drive unlocked.

A blank screen blinked to life.

Then folders began to appear, one after the other in rapid succession:

ASSET INDEX

PROJECT HELIX

BLACK FLOW LEDGER

OFFSHORE NETWORKS

WYTON LOGS

At the top of the interface, a line of stark white text:

CLASSIFIED – HELIX LEVEL 7 ACCESS –
EYES ONLY

SHADOW DIRECTIVE | LONDON – MOSCOW –
GENEVA

Alex leaned in. "What the hell is all this?"

Nikolai didn't answer. His face had hardened.

He clicked into the first file: Asset Index.

It was a database, hundreds of names. Agents. Informants. Operatives. Some flagged ACTIVE, others RETIRED, ROGUE, or COMPROMISED. Each name came with notes: dates, codenames, mission summaries. Cross-referenced with countries, timelines, and shockingly private sector clients.

Many of them weren't working for nations anymore.

They were working for *contracts*.

Corporations. Interests. Anonymous buyers.

Alex pointed at one of the entries.

"Is that Clive Ashburn? Dad used to mention him. Said he was a mentor. Trusted him."

Nikolai clicked the name.

A dossier appeared.

ASHBURN, CLIVE – MI6

Status: ACTIVE / CLASSIFIED / TIER BLACK

Note: Project Helix Liaison – London/Zurich/Ukraine Cell

Warning: Not to be contacted. May be under external pressure.

Alex swore under his breath. "So even the people he trusted weren't safe."

Nikolai opened the **Black Flow Ledger** next. It was far worse.

A comprehensive record of illegal arms transfers, drones, guided munitions, small arms, and more rerouted through humanitarian supply lines and diplomatic shipments.

"Here," Nikolai said, pointing. "This is how they keep the war alive. Both sides are being fed. Every battle is fuel for someone's bank account."

He clicked through dozens of entries, names of fake logistics companies and movement reports. One location was highlighted repeatedly.

"Wyton," Alex said. "That's in the UK. My dad took me past it once when I was a kid. Said it had ghosts."

"Maybe he wasn't being poetic," Nikolai muttered.

The final file was the one that chilled them both.

Project Helix.

Dozens of internal memos, cables, and heavily redacted assessments. One phrase kept appearing:

Kestrel Protocol activated. Directive: destabilisation through persistence warfare. Profitable tension. Multi-front shadow conflicts.

"Helix isn't just intelligence," Nikolai whispered. "It's a system. A *mechanism* for permanent war. Controlled. Monetised. Managed from the shadows."

Alex sank onto the couch, hand over his mouth. "And Dad was trying to dismantle it."

Nikolai nodded. "Alone. With no backup. He knew if he went to MI6, they'd silence him. If he went to the press, he'd be discredited or dead before he finished his first sentence."

"So, he did what he always did," Alex said bitterly. "He disappeared into the dark and played both sides until one of them pulled the trigger."

They sat in silence, the weight of what they had discovered pressing down like the concrete walls around them.

Finally, Alex spoke.

"We need to get this out. Every name. Every deal. Every lie."

Nikolai looked at him. "That'll get us both killed."

"I know," Alex said. "But if we don't, then John Winters died for nothing."

Outside, the sky was a sickly orange from distant fires. The city had gone still again, like it was holding its breath for what came next.

Inside, the brothers stared at the screen.

They weren't running anymore.

They were going to fight.

Chapter 14: A Ghost from MI6

Kyiv was colder now, not just from the dropping temperature, but from the weight of what the brothers had uncovered.

The Microdrive burned a hole in Alex's mind. The names, the deals, the web of deceit. It wasn't theory anymore. It wasn't paranoia. It was real.

And it was dangerous.

They needed someone who could verify what they'd seen, someone who wasn't dead or compromised.

Someone John had trusted.

That name had already surfaced: Clive Ashburn.

MI6 veteran. Analyst. A man John had once described as *"sharp enough to see the knife before it slips between your ribs."*

Officially retired. Unofficially... not quite.

They found him in an empty library annex near Shevchenkivskyi Park, arranged through a burner number hidden in one of John's encrypted files. The instructions had been brutally clear: come alone, no weapons, no surveillance. Clive would know if they broke the rules, and he would vanish.

Alex and Nikolai entered the crumbling reading room just before dusk. The place smelled of mildew, old leather bindings, and damp stone. Dust hung in the air like fog, and faded shelves loomed like sentinels in the gloom. Most of the overhead lights were dead, leaving the room in a bruised half-light. Only a single desk lamp glowed at the far end, casting a narrow cone of yellow across a table.

Beneath it sat a man, still as a statue.

Clive wore a charcoal wool coat tailored with military precision, collar turned up against the cold. His salt-and-pepper hair was neatly cut; his beard trimmed to officer regulation length. He had the lean, angular frame of a man who never fully retired, wiry, deliberate, dangerous. A faint scar traced his left cheekbone, a memory from an old war no one talked about anymore. His gloves were black leather, immaculate, and his eyes, when they finally lifted from the book, were grey and unreadable, like glass behind a firing slit.

He closed the book softly, as if it were a detonator, and let it rest on the table with care.

"You're early," he said without smiling. His voice was precise, devoid of accent, cultured in tone but honed like a blade.

"And that tells me two things," he added, motioning them forward with a flick of his fingers. "You're serious. And you're scared."

Alex didn't respond. But he felt it, the quiet, unblinking gravity of a man who had seen the worst and learned to live just fine with it.

"Alexander," he said, softly. "You have your father's eyes."

Alex didn't reply.

Nikolai stood silently at his side, arms crossed, watching Clive like a wolf studies an old rival.

"And you must be the other son. John told me about you, once. Said you had your mother's steel. I suppose we all inherit what we can."

"Why are you here?" Nikolai asked flatly.

Clive leaned back in his chair. "Because I owed John. Because I warned him *not* to do what he did. And because he never listened."

He glanced between them.

"And now you're both carrying what got him involved."

Alex pulled the flash drive from his pocket and placed it on the table. "He was trying to expose something. Project Helix. Black Flow. Wyton. Offshore accounts. Your name is in there."

Clive didn't flinch. "Of course it is. I helped build the original framework. Back when we thought it was about controlling chaos, not profiting from it."

He looked directly at Alex.

"Your father went too far. Not because he was wrong. But because he tried to take it down alone. You can't fight a machine from the inside without being chewed up by it."

Alex's voice was low. "He said someone had to."

Clive nodded. "He always believed in lost causes."

Nikolai stepped forward. "Who runs it now?"

Clive exhaled slowly, as if deciding whether to lie.

"No one runs it. That's what makes it so dangerous. Helix was built to be leaderless, a multi-lateral, multinational directive, funded through deniable assets and operated through front networks. Britain, Russia, Turkey, even Germany, all with stakes. No oversight. No accountability."

He leaned in.

"And now it's off the leash. Half the people still benefiting from it don't even know what it is anymore. They just follow the money."

Alex shook his head. "And Wyton?"

"A logistics hub. Originally used during the Balkans to move illegal arms under NATO cover. It was shut down, on paper. But the contractors never left. They just changed uniforms."

Nikolai's eyes narrowed. "So, who gave the kill order?"

Clive paused.

"There is no formal order anymore. Just triggers. John was marked the moment he accessed the original Helix data bank. MI6 was watching him. So were others. But my guess? The shot came from outside London. Someone farther east."

"Russia?" Alex asked.

Clive smiled darkly. "Russia has its hands in the pie, yes. But they're not the only ones hungry."

Silence fell.

Clive leaned back and looked at both of them with tired eyes.

"I warned him," he said again. "Told him to walk away. But John couldn't. Not when he found out what Wyton was being used for. Not when he found out the man running logistics was someone he trained."

Alex's blood turned cold. "Who?"

Clive hesitated. "A codename: **Kestrel**. No real name in the drive, I'm guessing?"

Nikolai shook his head. "Just a sealed envelope."

Clive's voice dropped to almost a whisper. "Then that's your next move."

He stood up slowly, adjusting the buttons on his coat.

"One more thing," he said. "Don't send that data out in bulk. It's too dangerous, too traceable. But if you want to break them, really break them, you'll need to give it to someone *inside* the system who still believes in the truth."

Alex narrowed his eyes. "You?"

Clive smiled faintly. "God, no. I'm a ghost, son. You need someone with teeth. Someone who still walks into the briefing rooms."

He dropped a card on the table.

"Her name's Sarah Lane. Investigative journalist but once an intelligence officer. Protected by whistleblower law, for now. Your father kept her safe once. Maybe she can return the favour."

He stood up and turned to leave.

"Tell her," he said over his shoulder, "that the shadows have teeth. And Kestrel flies high."

Then he was gone.

Alex looked down at the card.

Nikolai looked at him. "What now?"

Alex slipped the flash drive back into his pocket.

"Now," he said, "we find Kestrel."

Chapter 15: The Kestrel Envelope

They left the library through the back exit, no streetlamps, no foot traffic, just cracked paving stones and the faint hum of the city beyond.

Alex felt it first. The prickle. That sensation in the back of the neck that his father used to call "the second heartbeat." The instinct that someone, somewhere, was watching.

Nikolai felt it too. He stopped mid-step and scanned the rooftop line behind them.

Three floors up, movement.

"Don't look. Don't run," he muttered.

Alex's voice was taut. "You see it?"

"Two figures. One spotter, one with a comms unit. Surveillance team. Professional."

They walked on in silence another fifty metres. Then Nikolai grabbed Alex's arm and whispered, "Left. Now."

They ducked into a narrow alleyway, then veered again into a collapsed courtyard behind a boarded-up bakery. Shadows pressed in around them, and for a moment, the city swallowed them whole.

Footsteps followed. Soft. Measured.

Then a voice, distant but amplified by something synthetic, comms.

"Targets in motion. Confirmed ID on both. Orders confirmed, keep them breathing, until we confirm the drive is secured."

Nikolai swore in Russian.

Alex's breath caught. "They're not here to kill us. Not yet."

"Which means they will," Nikolai snapped, "once they have what they want."

He yanked open a loose grate leading to an old maintenance tunnel, the sort of thing every city has but few remember.

"In," he said.

They slipped into the dark.

They emerged five blocks later, behind an abandoned theatre. No footsteps. No voices. They had shaken them for now.

Back at the safe flat, Alex slammed the bolt shut and leaned against the door, chest heaving.

"They were military," he said. "Private contractors?"

"Could be Helix assets. Could be government. Doesn't matter," Nikolai said. "They want the drive. And they want us gone."

He opened his pack, pulled out the sealed envelope marked *Kestrel Protocol*, and laid it on the table between them.

It had waited long enough.

The envelope was heavy.

Inside, folded neatly, were three items:

- A redacted MI6 field report stamped *EYES ONLY*
- A Polaroid photograph
- A handwritten note, unmistakably John's handwriting

Nikolai read it aloud:

Kestrel isn't a code. It's a person.

Real name: Sarah Lane doesn't know. But she's seen him, and she'll remember his voice. He was her handler once. Mine too, for a while. But he chose power over principle. If you're reading this, he's either already silenced me or tried to.

He's embedded. British, but connected to all sides. He doesn't pull strings. He burns the puppets and blames the fire on someone else.

Do not confront him until you understand what he is protecting. He will not hesitate to kill you both.
Find Lane. Trust no one else.

Alex picked up the Polaroid. It showed a man in his early fifties, white shirt and blazer, standing outside a London government building, mid-conversation. His face was sharp, eyes hollow. Unmemorable and somehow deeply unsettling.

"He looks like no one," Alex murmured.

"Exactly," Nikolai said. "The perfect face to hide the worst intentions."

Alex scanned the MI6 report, most of it was blacked out. But one phrase stood out:

Subject: Kestrel. Authorisation for tactical misinformation campaign approved. All assets deniable. Termination protocols active if compromise risk exceeds 14%.

Alex looked up. "He's not just an operator. He's the failsafe."

Nikolai stared at the photo.

"There's something else," he said. "Those men today, they weren't amateurs. One of them had a throat tattoo. Cyrillic letters."

Alex raised an eyebrow. "You recognise it?"

Nikolai nodded grimly. "It's from a mercenary group. Ex-Spetsnaz. Exiled. Paid well. Rumoured to take freelance orders from Western clients when their hands need to stay clean."

Alex stared at the Kestrel photograph. So, we're dealing with a ghost, protected by mercs, sanctioned by someone high up, and tied to a global arms network."

Nikolai glanced at the drive on the desk.

"He wants that burned. And if we disappear, no one will ever know this existed."

Silence settled like dust.

Then Alex spoke, his voice quiet but firm.

"We need to find Sarah Lane."

"She's in the UK," Nikolai said. "You really think we can get out of Kyiv with that thing still tracking us?"

"No," Alex said. "But I think we can *draw him out*."

Nikolai looked at him.

"You want to bait the Kestrel."

Alex nodded.

"We leak something small. Something true. Something personal to him. Let him come to us."

Nikolai's eyes narrowed. "Dangerous."

Alex met his gaze.

"So was our father."

Chapter 16: The Bait

Alex sat at the edge of the desk, laptop open, eyes flicking between fragments of the data they'd recovered, names, wire transfers, operations with codenames that sounded like myths. *Blackflow. Mirrorhand. Helix.*

"Kestrel won't run," Nikolai said from the window, watching the street below through a slice in the curtain. "He's too confident. Men like that don't flinch. They hunt."

"Good," Alex replied. "Let him think we're prey."

They drafted a short, calculated leak.

No major names. No full document dumps. Just a few carefully chosen pieces of truth: a photo showing marked containers on a civilian aircraft. A redacted page showing the Helix program had been revived. And a single line in a now-deleted forum:

Kestrel is active. We have the drive. Come and get it.

They uploaded it through a secure, burnable relay channel tied to an old journalist network John once used in the Balkans.

Then they waited.

The response was faster than expected.

Within four hours, the safe flat's internet connection flickered then dropped completely. Cell signals vanished. Across the street, a parked van that had been there for days suddenly drove away. Moments later, a drone passed low over the roof, too quiet, too precise.

"They're triangulating," Nikolai muttered. "Not Helix field assets. This is corporate. Cleaners."

Alex stared out the window, jaw tight. "Which means Kestrel's watching."

"But not here," Nikolai added. "Not yet."

They both knew that wouldn't last.

That night, while sweeping the room for surveillance gear, Nikolai found something wedged behind the baseboard under the desk. A loose floor tile. Carefully hidden.

He pried it open.

Inside, wrapped in plastic and velvet cloth, was a small encrypted hard drive, different from the others.

Alex recognized the insignia on the casing: a stylised falcon etched in fading gold.

"I've seen this before," he said, voice low. "In my dad's study. He always kept it locked up."

They connected it to the laptop.

There was only one file.

TO ALEXANDER AND NIKOLAI — IN THE EVENT OF MY DEATH

They stared at the screen. Then Alex clicked play.

John Winters appeared, seated at a table in a dimly lit room. He looked older. Tired. Worn by time and weight. His hair was greyer, his eyes sunken, but clear.

He started with a long silence.

Then:

"If you're watching this, it means I didn't make it. And the secrets I tried to carry alone have finally fallen into your hands."

"I spent my life walking through shadows. I convinced myself it was for the greater good. Maybe it was, once. But eventually… the lines blur. You start to believe you're still the man who joined to do the right thing. You forget who you've become."

"Helix wasn't just a project. It was a disease. It infected everything, truth, loyalty, justice. I tried to shut it down from the inside. I failed. And people died."

"I was never a good father. I told myself I was protecting you. But what I really did was abandon you. Both of you."

He looked straight into the camera then, voice raw.

"Alex… you were my light. The part of me that never touched the job. I kept you in the dark because I thought it would keep you safe. I see now that safety without truth is its own kind of prison."

"Nikolai… you were my blood, too. I left you behind in a country that would eat you alive. And you survived. Not because of me. But in spite of me. And I have never been prouder or more ashamed."

"I am not asking you to forgive me. I am asking you to finish what I couldn't."

"But only together."

He paused, a silence thick with regret.

"Kestrel will come. He'll try to buy you, then break you, then erase you. Do not let him divide you. That's how he wins. That's how *they* all win."

"Burn it. Leak it. Kill it. Or bury it. The choice is yours. But whatever you do, do it together."

"Truth is the last safehouse. Don't let it fall."

The screen went black.

Neither brother spoke for several minutes.

The silence was heavy, not from shock, but from something deeper. A sadness they hadn't let themselves feel until now.

Alex looked at Nikolai.

"For so long, I thought I hated him," he said. "Turns out I never even knew him."

Nikolai's voice was low. "We both did."

He looked at the laptop. "But now we do."

At that moment, the apartment lights flickered. Then cut out.

Power gone.

Down the hall, footsteps.

Nikolai moved quickly, pulling Alex behind the kitchenette wall. Through the peephole, he saw them: three men, dressed as civilians but moving like trained operators, approaching from the stairwell quiet, deliberate, armed.

"Kestrel's calling card," Nikolai whispered.

Alex opened his pack and removed the flash drive. "What do we do?"

"We vanish."

Chapter 17: Into the Shadows

The hallway outside erupted into quiet violence.

A suppressed shot punched through the air. Splintered wood burst from the doorframe just inches from Alex's head.

Nikolai yanked him backwards, knocking over the kitchenette table as they scrambled into the bedroom. "They're breaching."

Alex grabbed the encrypted hard drives, stuffing them into his pack while Nikolai jammed a chair under the handle.

"We've got two minutes, max," Nikolai muttered, already moving toward the window. "They don't want survivors. Just silence."

A drone buzzed past outside, the same low, wasp-like whine they'd heard before.

"Not the front," Alex said. "They'll have both exits covered."

"Then we make our own."

Nikolai pulled a screwdriver from his coat and began prying loose the vent panel above the window. Behind it, a narrow shaft, tight, but passable.

"Help me up," he said.

Ten minutes later, bruised and breathless, they emerged three buildings over in a back alley behind a silent tram station.

The rain had returned, heavier now. The streets glistened in the orange wash of distant fires and flickering streetlights.

They moved fast.

Through old maintenance tunnels and half-demolished service corridors, they slipped beneath the surface of Kyiv, hunted, anonymous, untraceable. They switched coats, disposed of their old IDs, and made contact with one of Danylo's people a former border guard who owed John a debt that couldn't be repaid with words.

By sunrise, they were moving, disguised in an aid transport convoy heading west, to collect supplies and no questions asked.

It took two days to reach the Polish border.

Two days of rotating sleep, backroad detours, and the creeping dread that they were still being watched.

At the crossing near Medyka, they didn't breathe easy until they were waved through by a young customs officer with tired eyes and a distracted glance.

Safe, for now.

The border morgue in Rzeszów was cold and bureaucratic, the kind of place where even grief felt regulated.

John Winters' body still lay in stasis under a false identity. The British embassy had issued a hold. Questions. Suspicions. Allegiances still uncertain.

But Nikolai had planned ahead.

He met the head of the facility an older Polish man named Dr. Marek Gwiazda, in the back office late that night. No forms. No cameras.

Just a briefcase.

Inside: €10,000 in clean cash scraped together from a series of offshore transfers Nikolai had decrypted from the Helix account trails. Dirty money, stolen from the very system that had killed their father.

Marek opened the case, nodded once, and slid over a cremation release form stamped "Diplomatic Transfer."

"No records," Marek said. "He'll be marked as repatriated on humanitarian grounds. Nobody asks questions when the British don't want to answer them."

Nikolai stared at the man. "That's the most honest thing I've heard in weeks."

Three days later, they stepped off a quiet flight into Manchester Airport, arriving on forged emergency passports under an NHS repatriation scheme.

No fanfare. No reception. Just drizzle on the tarmac and a horizon full of unanswered questions.

They rented a car and drove north through the wet grey sprawl of the city, the ash-urn secured in the back seat, wrapped in cloth, heavy with silence.

Neither spoke much.

Not until they reached the small churchyard on the edge of the Peak District, the one John had once told Alex he wanted to be buried near, though he'd never explained why.

"'Where the trees see the wind before it comes,'" Alex muttered, repeating the phrase John had once said during a rare moment of openness.

Nikolai simply nodded. "He chose well."

The spreading of Johns Ashes was private.

No officials. No ceremony. Just the two brothers

Nikolai placed a single stone atop the fresh soil, an old Russian tradition. "Rest, *otets*. We'll carry the rest."

That night, they sat in the back of a quiet pub near the station, nursing warm beer and cold thoughts.

"We could run," Alex said. "Leave the drive in a vault. Let someone else pick up the pieces."

Nikolai shook his head. "You saw what Kestrel did just to keep it quiet. If we don't act, someone else dies."

Alex looked at the flash drive on the table. "So, what now?"

Nikolai reached into his coat and pulled out the card John had left them, Sarah Lane.

He placed it beside the drive.

"She's next."

Chapter 18: The Journalist

The café sat tucked between a disused post office and a boarded-up newsagent on a quiet Manchester city Centre Street. Rain streaked the windowpane as the city went about its ordinary business, commuters, school runs, umbrellas opening and closing like soft weapons.

Alex stirred his coffee but didn't drink it. Nikolai sat across from him, arms folded, eyes on the door. Neither had slept more than a few hours since scattering their dads' ashes

At exactly 11:00 a.m., she arrived.

Sarah Lane.

Late-forties, greying at the temples, dressed in jeans, a long coat, and trainers that had seen better days. No makeup but still attractive. No small talk. She walked in like someone who didn't trust the room, ordered black tea, then slid into the booth beside them without a word.

"You're Alex," she said, looking him dead in the eye. "He told me about you."

Then her gaze shifted to Nikolai. "And you're the surprise."

Nikolai smirked faintly. "I get that a lot."

Sarah glanced down at the plain USB drive Alex had placed on the table.

"You know how many of these I've been shown over the years?" she asked. "Half of them are clickbait. The other half are suicide notes."

Alex leaned in. "This one got our father killed."

Sarah didn't blink. "Then you'll understand why I'm not just going to plug it into my laptop and cross my fingers."

Nikolai slid a folder across the table. Inside were printouts: redacted asset files, satellite manifests from

Wyton, and several names she would know, people once praised in the press, now exposed as ghosts on a black payroll.

"I decrypted these myself," he said. "We haven't released the full contents yet. But we need a journalist contact who understands the system and knows how not to trip the alarm."

Sarah scanned the documents, her expression neutral but intent. The fingers on her teacup stilled when she reached one specific name.

"I know this man," she said. "He was flagged in the inquiry into arms transfers to Syria. Quietly acquitted. MI6 buried the real charges."

Alex nodded. "He's still active. The program never stopped. It just changed its name. Project Helix."

Sarah closed the folder slowly. Her voice dropped a level.

"Do you have *proof* this is real? Not just files, but verification? Dates, metadata, original source trail?"

"Yes," Alex said. "And we can trace the funding. From front companies to accounts. Even to Wyton. You just need to tell us where to start."

She sat back, arms crossed.

"I'm not stupid. If what you're showing me is even *half* true, you're both walking targets."

"We know," Nikolai said.

"Good," she replied, standing up. "Then you'll understand why I won't go anywhere near this unless I see the full data, metadata tags, original comms logs, and encryption certificates. I need *everything*. And if it checks out... I'll take it global."

Alex stood too. "What if it doesn't?"

Sarah gave him a hard look. "Then I'll Walk. And you'll both disappear buried in a two-line article about 'accidental deaths overseas.'"

Later that night, in a secure co-working space Sarah arranged through a journalist's protection fund, they plugged the master copy of the drive into a fresh, isolated machine. No internet. No wireless.

Sarah worked silently.

An hour passed. Then two.

Then she pushed back from the screen, slowly.

"It's real," she said. "Not just real, it's devastating. This will crush careers, ruin governments, and light up half of Europe's security community."

She looked at Alex. "And Kestrel?"

"We have a photo. A field report. And John's warning. It's not a name. It's a position. A role passed down when needed."

Sarah nodded grimly. "Then we don't go at him directly. We go at his *influence*. We dismantle the system first."

Nikolai looked at her. "You're in?"

She closed the laptop gently.

"I'm in."

Back outside, the city breathed easy again. Rain had stopped. Pigeons lined the rooftops. Normal life moved on, unaware of the war happening just below the surface.

Alex looked over at Nikolai as they stepped into the cold.

"She's the first person that doesn't feel like a ghost," he said.

Nikolai nodded. "Then let's give her something to haunt them with."

Chapter 19: The Trap

They chose a name from the drive.

One they were sure would bite.

Leon Radek a Czech-born logistics specialist turned covert asset handler, listed under Helix Tier 3. Former military. Now tied to several black-market arms movements across Ukraine and the Balkans. John's notes had highlighted him twice: once in red, and again with the words *"Unstable. Sloppy under pressure."*

Perfect.

In the days since Sarah Lane joined them, they'd moved carefully building the framework of an information leak that wouldn't cause panic but would start tremors in the right corridors.

They had already released fragments of the Wyton logs and a blurred image of a shipment loaded onto an aid-marked truck. Independent journalists picked it up. Analysts began whispering.

But that wasn't enough.

They needed *confession*. They needed a name on camera. Someone inside the machine admitting it was real.

They needed Radek.

The bait was simple: a fake buyer, carefully placed in a secure chat forum frequented by black-market brokers. Sarah used one of John's old identities to request "access to discreet tactical shipping routes in Eastern Europe," citing business with a Turkish intermediary. The digital footprint was convincing enough to get Radek's attention.

Within days, he reached out under the alias "K3Wolf".

The location was neutral ground: a hotel bar in Brussels, posing as a transport meeting between rival buyers. Public enough to avoid a hit. Private enough for dirty words to flow.

The hotel bar in Brussels was dimly lit, all dark mahogany and soft jazz, the kind of place that masked tired eyes and whispered conversations. Alex sat with his back to the mirrored wall, nursing a short glass of scotch, the amber liquid catching the low light like fire trapped in glass. Across from him, Nikolai stirred an untouched espresso, eyes scanning the room out of habit, the tension in his shoulders never quite leaving. A modified phone sat on the table, streaming directly to Sarah's laptop two floors up.

Radek arrived ten minutes late.

Leather jacket. Cheap cologne. Eyes like a man who'd learned how to watch for ghosts.

"Mr. Harland?" he said, looking at Nikolai.

"Depends who's asking," Nikolai replied.

Radek grinned. "You asked about payload routes to Moldova. I can open doors, but doors cost."

Alex leaned in. "We're not paying unless we know who's signing off on them."

Radek took the bait.

He leaned in closer, the grin still there. "You're cute. You think these routes exist without approval?"

"Whose approval?" Nikolai asked calmly.

Radek chuckled, clearly enjoying the moment. "Ministry of Defence officials in the UK, contractors in Lithuania, back-channel payments from Polish logistics firms. Hell, even some Ukrainians skim off the top. It's all sanctioned. As long as the reports say the aid got there, nobody asks where the rifles ended up."

He took a sip of his drink, then added: "You know what we call this business? *Order through instability*. It's beautiful. Never-ending demand."

Alex gave a slight nod. "Got everything," he whispered, barely moving his lips.

They didn't wait to finish their drinks.

Within ten minutes, Radek was back in the bar, and Alex and Nikolai were halfway to the secure upload site Sarah had prepared in advance.

The confession, in full HD was uploaded to three locations, watermarked with time, date, and Radek's visible face. Two independent reporters received it anonymously with corroborating files from the Helix drive.

By morning, it was everywhere.

The Guardian ran it first:

"Explosive Video Reveals Arms Trafficking Network Tied to Western Intelligence."

Then Der Spiegel, then a mid-level defence whistleblower came forward anonymously to confirm elements of the network's existence. It was enough to ignite interest but not enough to trigger full-scale panic.

Just the right amount of flame.

But the fire had only just begun.

Kestrel responded within 48 hours.

Not with bullets.

With silence.

Sarah's secure flat in Manchester was broken into while she was away. No files stolen. Nothing touched.

Except for one item.

On her desk, they left a single feather, grey, bloodied and a copy of her first published article folded neatly on her keyboard.

No fingerprints. No prints at all.

Just a message.

"They're watching us," Alex said, pacing the small hallway while Sarah stared at the feather. "He's letting us know."

Nikolai checked the building cameras. "Everything was looped. They walked right through."

Sarah didn't look up. "He's telling us he's not scared."

Nikolai nodded grimly. "Then we make him scared."

Chapter 20: The Decision

The storm rolled over Manchester like a slow drumbeat, wind lashing the windows of the small safe flat. Lightning pulsed behind the clouds, illuminating the room in brief flashes, bursts of white over grey concrete and darker thoughts.

The brothers sat opposite each other, the flickering glow of Sarah's encrypted laptop casting long shadows across the floor.

On the screen: everything.

The complete Helix archive.

Names, assets, payments, terminal orders, field deaths disguised as accidents, backdoor arms deals routed through fake charities, and false humanitarian airlifts carrying munitions into conflict zones under international logos.

The full, unredacted truth.

Alex rubbed his face with both hands. He looked exhausted not just physically, but morally. Worn down by the sheer weight of what they held.

"We can't just dump it," he said. "It's too much. There are names in here of people who were used people who thought they were doing good. We release this, we don't just burn the guilty. We destroy the innocent."

Nikolai leaned forward, arms on his knees, staring hard at the screen. "And if we *don't* release it all, the machine keeps turning. You think surgical strikes will cripple this? They'll absorb it. Adapt. Retaliate."

"This isn't war, Nikolai. It's a scalpel, not a grenade."

"No," Nikolai snapped. "It *is* a war. One our father fought with shadows and lies and look where it got him."

Alex shot him a glare. "He died trying to stop this, not scorch the world."

"Exactly," Nikolai said, leaning closer. "He died being *careful*. Playing chess while they played with fire. We need to be louder."

Silence.

Only the wind outside, and the quiet hum of the hard drive spinning.

Sarah stood in the doorway, watching them both. She hadn't spoken in ten minutes, just listened. Now she stepped in and placed a small stack of printouts on the table.

"Leaking everything burns the house down," she said. "But doing nothing keeps the rot hidden in the walls. There's a third way."

They looked at her.

She flipped through the papers. "We target key figures. Verified, provable, undeniably complicit. We drop only what we can back up *publicly*. No grey areas. No collateral."

She looked at Alex. "You don't want innocent lives ruined."

Then at Nikolai. "You want impact."

"Do it in phases," she said. "Expose, isolate, collapse."

Alex leaned back slowly, thinking.

Nikolai stared at the drive. Then finally, a quiet nod.

"We start with Wyton. Then the funding routes. The ghost accounts. The ministers who signed the off-book approvals."

Alex hesitated, then reached for the laptop. "And Kestrel?"

Sarah didn't flinch. "We don't name him yet. But we shine a light into his corner. Force him out."

The decision was made.

They began that night, building the first curated data drop with timestamps, signatures, transfer orders, and delivery manifests. Names tied directly to illicit activity, verified against external records.

Sarah reached out to three vetted journalists across Europe, ones with integrity, reach, and enough paranoia to stay alive.

By dawn, the documents were in their hands, with timed releases scheduled over the next seven days.

And just like that the first stone dropped into the pond.

Alex stood by the window, arms crossed.

"We could've gone the other way."

Nikolai stood beside him. "We still might have to."

"Do you think he'd be proud of this?" Alex asked.

Nikolai didn't answer right away. Then: "I think he'd be proud we did it *together*."

They stood there, watching the rain streak the glass, two sons of a ghost, reshaping the storm he left behind.

Chapter 21: Sons of a Traitor

The headline hit like a bomb.

BREAKING: MI6 Source Tied to Rogue Agent John Winters Claims "Years of Espionage" for Russia and Ukraine

Underneath it: a still image of John Winters in a military facility, grainy and cropped, sitting beside a Russian general and a man in Ukrainian militia fatigues. The caption below was damning.

"Unseen until now: classified footage allegedly shows the disgraced former operative coordinating unauthorized weapons shipments from both Russian and Ukrainian handlers during 2017–2022. Source within British intelligence confirms ongoing investigation into treason allegations."

Alex stared at the screen, frozen. His face had gone pale.

Nikolai slowly rose from the sofa, eyes narrowing. "That's a deepfake," he muttered. "It has to be."

Sarah Lane, still at her laptop in the corner, was already running the footage through her verification software. She didn't look up. "It's good. Really good. But I can already see the seams. The lighting doesn't match. Shadows are wrong. Voice modulation's perfect, too perfect."

She clicked the mouse, scrubbing through the footage again. "They used archival interviews, layered over facial animation. The military insignia on the Russian officer it's obsolete. Retired in 2016. This is manufactured."

Alex sat down hard, still staring at the screen.

Dozens of articles were already circulating. Politico, Euronews, Sky. Even Reuters was hedging:

"Unverified footage suggests John Winters may have been involved in unauthorized intelligence transfers. The allegations follow

the leak of controversial documents tied to a shadow program codenamed 'Helix.'"

"They're not denying the leak," Sarah said. "They're reframing it. Undermining the source. Make John a traitor, and the rest collapses under suspicion."

Nikolai's jaw clenched. "Classic counter-intel tactic. Create noise. Divide loyalties. Muddy the water until truth drowns."

He turned to Alex. "If we're the sons of a traitor, no one will listen. Everything we leaked, everything Dad gave us, it'll be seen as manipulation. Enemy propaganda."

Alex's voice cracked. "And people will believe it."

Six hours later, the knock came at the door.

Sharp. Three raps. Then silence.

Sarah froze.

Nikolai was already moving, silent against the floorboards. He peeked through the peephole. Then relaxed slightly.

"Danylo," he said, unlocking the door.

The Ukrainian resistance fighter stepped in, soaked from rain, eyes hard.

"I saw the broadcasts," he said. "Your father's face on every screen between here and Kyiv. You need to know: it's spreading. Fast. People believe it. Even inside the circles I trust."

He looked at Nikolai. "I've already had to shut down two of our safehouses. Someone's feeding false alerts to Ukrainian intelligence. You've been flagged as Russian-aligned operatives."

Nikolai looked at Sarah. "They're burning our cover."

Sarah closed her laptop and stood.

"We either go dark or we go loud," she said. "But either way, we're out of time."

That night, Sarah drafted a public response, carefully worded. Denial wasn't enough, they needed to dismantle the lie piece by piece. She included metadata from the original Helix drive, digital forensics of the deepfake, and historical inconsistencies in the footage timeline.

It wasn't a bombshell, not like the leak but it was enough to sow doubt.

She posted it under her own name.

And within minutes, *she* was trending.

Back in the flat, Alex sat alone with a photo of his father, the real one taken in the garden years ago. Sunlight on his face. No secrets. Just a man with his sleeves rolled up, a rare smile on his lips.

Now the world thought that man was a traitor.

"You knew this would happen, didn't you?" he whispered. "You knew they'd paint you in shadows."

From behind him, Nikolai spoke quietly.

"He wasn't perfect. He did things. Ugly things. But he never stopped trying to make it mean something."

Alex looked up. "Then we do the same."

Nikolai gave a single nod. "But not here. Not now. We need to move."

"To where?"

"Back to the beginning," Nikolai said. "Where Helix was born."

Sarah stepped back into the room, her coat already on.

"You mean London."

"No," Nikolai said. "Before that."

He turned to them both, eyes cold and clear. "*Zurich.*"

Chapter 22: The Offer

The message arrived encrypted, invisible to normal networks routed through a disposable device Alex hadn't even taken out of its foil wrapping since Poland. The phone blinked once. No ringtone. No vibration. Just a pale green screen with a single word:

"Accept."

He showed it to Nikolai and Sarah. No one spoke.

Sarah narrowed her eyes. "Whoever sent that knew how to bypass three layers of onion routing."

Nikolai tilted the screen. "And they know we're in Zurich."

The phone pinged again. A second message loaded automatically, coordinates, followed by two chilling details:

PRIVATE JET. GENEVA. 18:00.

NO TRACKING. NO QUESTIONS. BLANK SLATE.

Then:

"We don't care about Kestrel. We care about Helix. You hold the keys. Let's talk."

They met the jet at a private hangar at Geneva Cointrin. It sat under armed security and polished lights, a sleek, white Gulfstream with no tail markings and two stewards who said nothing as they were ushered aboard.

Inside: leather seats, silent engines, and a woman already waiting.

She wore no badge. No security team. Just a charcoal-grey pantsuit and calm, calculated confidence.

"I'm Emilia Locke," she said as they sat. "Director of Special Risk for *Argus Directive Group*."

Sarah's breath caught. "I've heard of Argus. Private intel firm. Mostly myth."

Emilia smiled faintly. "Most good intelligence is."

She gestured to a leather folder already laid open on the table. Inside: a contract with no company header, a sum of £8.5 million, and a digital certificate promising full immunity from prosecution under a shell entity based in the Cayman Islands.

"The deal is simple," she said. "We acquire the Helix drive. You disappear. Comfortably. Safely. We bury the rest."

Nikolai scoffed. "So, you can weaponize it for leverage."

Emilia didn't flinch. "Weaponization is inevitable. You might as well choose who pulls the trigger."

Alex leaned forward. "What are you, really? A mercenary, CIA? A hedge fund with blackmail?"

Emilia's smile disappeared. "We are realists. Helix is not just intelligence. It's access. People. Assets. Programs that could collapse markets, erode alliances. In the wrong hands, it's chaos. But in *ours*, it's... balance."

Sarah crossed her arms. "Control, you mean."

"I mean deterrence," Emilia replied coldly. "The truth doesn't set anyone free. It destabilizes. You think you're liberators. But all you'll do is start a fire that burns everything, including yourselves."

She folded the contract and placed it back into the leather sleeve.

"You have 48 hours," she said. "After that, the offer expires."

"Why?" Alex asked.

Emilia stood. "Because by then, the people you're running from will stop playing chess... and start playing war."

As the jet lifted off and disappeared into the low evening cloud, the three of them stood on the tarmac in silence.

Nikolai turned to Sarah. "Would you take it?"

Sarah's jaw was tight. "No. But I've seen people take far less for a lot more blood."

Alex looked out across the airfield, the city lights of Geneva glittering in the distance.

"They're not lying," he said quietly. "We *are* holding a fuse."

Nikolai looked at him. "Then we'd better decide who we light it under."

Chapter 23: The Mole

Zurich's morning air was razor-crisp, the sky hanging low and metallic above the lake. Alex stood on the balcony of their private apartment, staring out at the still water below, a mirror to his storming thoughts.

Inside, the argument was already escalating.

"We can't just *ignore* the offer," Sarah said. "If we walk away and they come after us, we're dead. All of us."

"They'll come after us *anyway*," Nikolai replied, voice firm but cold. "They don't want to buy Helix, they want to erase it. We're just part of the cleanup."

Alex turned, stepping back inside.

"You saw the money. The immunity. They want to own the narrative. Not silence it."

Sarah nodded. "And they already *are*. Look at the media shift in the last 24 hours. The headlines aren't about the leak anymore, they're about our *legitimacy*. Every time we try to push back, another story lands. It's too fast. Too precise."

Nikolai frowned. "Which means someone's feeding them."

A heavy silence fell.

Sarah's eyes narrowed. "You think we've been compromised?"

Alex crossed the room and opened his laptop. "We sent partial copies of the Helix data to three journalists for protection. Off-grid, encrypted. If the story's moving faster than our own leaks, then someone inside that circle is sharing intel."

He began typing furiously, pulling up the transfer logs.

"The packets were unique. I watermarked each set with minor timestamp variances, trackable to the millisecond."

Nikolai stepped closer. "Like digital fingerprints."

Alex's eyes scanned the list. He zoomed in. One line glowed red.

Packet C-002: Timestamp leak. Contact: Leo Varney.

Sarah's face froze. "No. Leo's solid. I've worked with him for many years. He's exposed defence contractors, Black River's mining fraud in Niger"

"And now he's working for Argus," Nikolai interrupted, voice quiet and certain.

Alex turned the screen. "Packet C-002 was copied twice. Once to his machine. Once, a few hours later, to a secure Argus node traced through a shell server in Malta."

Sarah stared at the screen, her jaw set.

"Son of a bitch."

Three hours later, they sat in a shuttered café in Zürich's Old Town, not for the coffee, but for the proximity to Leo's safe drop.

Sarah had called him that morning under the pretext of meeting for an emergency correction on the latest leak. He'd agreed immediately, with the same cool charm he always used.

He arrived ten minutes early.

Leather satchel. Long coat. Sunglasses too dark for the overcast day.

"You've been busy," he said, sliding into the booth. "London's on fire."

Sarah didn't waste time.

"How long, Leo?"

His smile faltered. "Excuse me?"

"Don't bother," Nikolai said. "We traced the packet."

Alex leaned in. "You sent our intel to Argus. The third copy. And you didn't even bother to reroute the metadata. Sloppy."

Leo's face dropped its act like a mask sliding from a shelf.

"I didn't have a choice," he said flatly. "They came to me. Said Helix wasn't a story; it was a geopolitical *weapon*. If I didn't help them contain it, they'd black bag me and pin it all on you."

Sarah stared at him, devastated. "You could have *told* me."

"And you would've dragged me into your mess," he snapped. "You were *right* to dig, Sarah. But you crossed a line. These people aren't government. They're beyond it."

Nikolai stood slowly. "So what now? They watching you? Are we marked?"

Leo swallowed. "Not yet. You've got time left before the Argus window closes. They still want the drive. If you disappear… they stop hunting."

Alex's voice was hollow. "But we don't disappear, do we?"

Leo shook his head. "No. You either sell out… or you go to war."

Back in the apartment, the trio sat in silence as the wind bumped against the windows, matching the pounding of Alex's heart.

He looked at Nikolai, then Sarah.

"We're out of time."

Sarah nodded, face drawn but resolute.

"Then we finish it," she said.

Nikolai stepped toward the laptop and brought up the final section of the Helix drive, the one marked "ARCHANGEL."

Alex asked, "What is that?"

Nikolai's expression darkened.

"Kestrel's final play."

Chapter 24: ARCHANGEL

Zurich's night skyline blinked with artificial calm, pristine, ordered and oblivious.

But in the hills beyond, beneath the glow of surveillance towers and wind turbines, an old communications facility nestled into the forest had quietly changed hands.

It now housed a Helix failsafe.

A black site vault.

And the last clue John Winters ever traced.

The plan was simple.

In and out in twelve minutes.

Get to the mainframe. Extract the ARCHANGEL files. Burn the backups.

The execution? Far messier.

Alex crouched beside Nikolai on the pine-needled slope above the compound's rear fence. Below, half a dozen armed guards walked perimeter rotations, flashlights cutting through fog like slow knives.

"Power grid's already been looped," Sarah's voice whispered through their earpieces. "Cameras blind in twenty seconds. Lights go in thirty. That's your window."

Alex's fingers flexed around the grip of his pistol. "Copy. Moving on zero."

Nikolai cracked his knuckles. "Time to knock."

At thirty seconds, the forest plunged into darkness.

Floodlights blinked out. Sirens gave a brief, startled squeal before going dead.

And then Alex and Nikolai were over the fence, ghosts in the night.

They moved fast, two shadows slicing across the gravel, up through a side entry door Nikolai lock-picked in seconds. Inside, emergency lights pulsed red and low.

Gunfire cracked from a hallway on their right, Helix guards reacting, but too late.

Nikolai dropped two in seconds.

Alex took a third with a clean shoulder shot, precise, not fatal. No time for guilt.

They moved through corridors of reinforced concrete, passing map rooms, and satellite uplinks still humming on backup batteries.

Then they reached the server vault.

Behind blast doors sat a singular terminal already active, still logged in. Someone had accessed it remotely moments before the blackout.

On the screen:

PROJECT: ARCHANGEL

Autonomous Strategic Satellite Response System

Status: ACTIVE

Failsafe Protocol: 72 HOURS TO GLOBAL SHADOW NET LINK

Alex blinked. "Oh my god…"

It wasn't just surveillance.

It was a *contingency weapon.*

ARCHANGEL was an AI-controlled orbital platform, once a NATO-funded defence tool, now hijacked by Helix. It controlled dormant autonomous drones, cyberwarfare capabilities, even experimental kinetic-strike satellites.

Failing secrecy? Trigger retaliation.

Kestrel's last card wasn't silence.

It was apocalypse by proxy.

Nikolai yanked the external drive from his belt and jammed it into the terminal.

"Copy it. Now."

A voice behind them.

"I wouldn't."

They turned, too late.

Two operators stepped from the corridor, rifles raised. Another came from the left, dragging a wounded guard.

"End of the road," one of them said, calm and smiling. "You're not the first rats to sniff this cheese. Just the last."

Gunfire exploded.

Nikolai dived behind a desk, Alex behind a toppled file cabinet.

The terminal sparked, hit in the first volley.

Alex gritted his teeth and returned fire, catching one in the thigh.

Then, pain.

A sharp, tearing heat through his upper arm. Blood soaked his jacket.

"Alex!" Nikolai shouted.

"I'm fine! Keep copying!"

One of the Helix men tried flanking. Nikolai met him with a brutal elbow and a point-blank shot. Another fell to Alex's fire, his hand trembling but steady.

Then the power died again, for good this time.

Darkness swallowed the room as Nikolia grabbed the drive.

They moved fast.

The rooftop escape plan was improvised up the rear stairwell, two more guards dropped in motion, adrenaline overriding exhaustion.

Outside, the night wind hit them hard. Sirens now screamed in the valley local police, drawn by the blackout.

Below, the woods swarmed with movement. Too many lights. Too many uniforms.

No more stealth.

"Move," Nikolai barked.

Alex stumbled hard, arm burning. But he was still moving.

The drive was intact.

They were alive.

Two hours later, coughing from the cold and covered in blood and sweat, they slid into the back of Sarah's van parked under a bridge just outside Bern.

"You got it?" she asked.

Nikolai nodded grimly, handing her the drive. "All of it."

She plugged it into a shielded laptop and opened the files.

Her face went pale.

"This is... *unimaginable*. ARCHANGEL isn't just Helix's insurance. It's a trigger system. If a final leak drops... it auto-deploys."

Alex leaned his head back, gasping. "So we can't leak it... without setting off a *war*?"

"No," Sarah said. "We *can*. But we need to kill the trigger first."

She turned, urgency in her voice. "We need to get back to London. Now."

As the van crossed into France under forged plates, Alex clutched his bandaged arm and stared out into the night.

They'd exposed Helix.

Survived an ambush.

Uncovered ARCHANGEL.

And now... they had to stop it, before the world burned under their father's unfinished shadow.

Chapter 25: Return to London

The Channel crossing was slow, silent, and full of dread.

Alex stared through the rain-streaked window of the ferry's lower deck, his wounded arm throbbing beneath the gauze. He barely noticed the rhythmic churn of the waves, all he could hear was John's voice, echoing in the back of his mind from the pre-recorded message they'd found days earlier:

"If you're watching this... I failed to stop it. But you can. Together."

Beside him, Nikolai sat with his eyes closed but his fingers twitching against his thigh. Sarah tapped rapidly on her laptop, connected through a scrambled relay to a dormant GCHQ server she'd cracked two years prior.

And then, her screen blinked.

A signal intercepted. Encrypted. Masked beneath layers of decoy traffic.

But unmistakably Helix.

The file was titled: OPERATION GLASSHOUSE.

Sarah froze. "They're accelerating the timeline."

"What is it?" Alex asked.

She turned the screen toward them.

Stage I: Coordinated drone strikes against RAF bases in Lossiemouth, Marham, and Brize Norton.

Stage II: Simultaneous disinformation leaks, doctored MI5 internal memos to be released by Russian-aligned proxy networks in Bulgaria and Moldova.

Stage III: Activations of three embedded sleeper assets inside the UK Defence Procurement Office, Home Office, and Porton Down.

"Jesus," Alex whispered. "It's not just retaliation... it's collapse."

Nikolai leaned closer. "They want to fracture trust in British military command, make it look like a breach from the inside. Tie it to Russian actors. And let the real architects Helix vanish in the smoke."

Sarah nodded grimly. "They'll pull out, liquidate assets, and resurface with clean hands in another country. The chaos gives them cover."

Alex clenched his jaw. "How long until the first stage?"

"According to these logs? A day or two max."

They crossed into Dover beneath darkness, slipping past border checks with forged IDs and a broken taillight that earned them a glance and a waved-through. From there, they stayed off the motorways, snaking their way through Kent and into the grey arteries of South London.

They didn't speak much.

But as the skyline of the city loomed ahead dark towers stabbed into mist and steel something shifted between the brothers.

Resolve.

They arrived at a nondescript safe house in Clapham just before dawn. It was another one of John's old dead-drops still untouched after all these years. Inside were dusty boxes of surveillance photos, encoded ledger books, burner phones, and a heavily protected briefcase locked with John's biometric print.

"Let me try something," Alex said.

He took the briefcase, placed his thumb on the scanner, and held his breath.

The light blinked once.

Then turned green.

Click.

Inside: A second, older hard drive. Heavier. With a torn handwritten label:

"Glasshouse / Counterfailsafe / Black Channel –
NOT TO BE TRUSTED."

Back on Sarah's laptop, the new drive decrypted
slowly. When it opened, what they found sent a chill
through the room.

John had anticipated Operation Glasshouse.

He had built a shadow map of it, names, phases,
trigger mechanisms, targets. But he had also uncovered a
counterplot: certain figures within UK and US Government
knew of the plan... and were choosing to let it happen.

Controlled damage or traitors.

A calculated "incident" to justify a sweeping new
intelligence directive across NATO more surveillance, more
spending, and privatised oversight under contracts linked
directly to Helix-affiliated firms.

Sarah's eyes went wide. "They're going to let the
first strike happen, so they can pass sweeping powers
afterward. It's a modern-day Reichstag fire."

Alex stood. "Then we stop it before it lights."

At 03:00, an anonymous message was sent through
a ghost contact in MI5: urgent intel regarding rogue drone
deployments and compromised internal systems. The
message was intercepted within six minutes, but no
response came back.

Sarah closed the laptop slowly.

"They've already compromised the response chain.
Our warning won't reach the right hands."

Nikolai reached for his coffee.

"Then we don't *warn*."

He looked at Alex.

"We act."

Next Objective: RAF Marham.
Strike window: 17 hours.

And Helix wasn't going to wait.

Chapter 26: Firebreak

The sky above RAF Marham was pale and moody, clouds dragging low over the Norfolk countryside like smoke trailing from some distant, unseen fire.

Alex and Nikolai stood at the public viewing area near the airfield's perimeter, an open field dotted with enthusiasts, photographers, and aviation buffs wrapped in jackets, sipping coffee from flasks, watching the F35 Lightnings and Voyagers taxi and take off.

But the brothers weren't there to plane-watch.

Alex scanned the far side of the base with binoculars, sweat prickling under his collar despite the chill. Nikolai, seated on a fold-up stool beside him, typed rapidly on a burner tablet connected to a high-gain signal antenna hidden in their rucksack.

"No signs of lockdown," Nikolai muttered. "No unusual flight pattern deviations. They're running full ops. They have *no idea* what's coming."

Alex's eyes flicked to the timer on his watch. T-minus 2 hours 14 minutes.

"We're running out of time," he said. "If those drones go live…"

Nikolai shook his head. "We're not breaching the base. We wouldn't make it ten feet before being face-down in the dirt."

"But we *can* make someone listen," Alex said grimly.

Nikolai looked around, noting a Royal Air Force sergeant casually chatting with a pair of cadets near the fence line. Too low in the food chain. They needed an officer someone *with clearance* and fast.

Back in London, Sarah Lane moved fast through the corridors of Portcullis House, ducking beneath the scaffolding of renovation works and security patrols.

Her contact minister Rachel Merrin, Secretary for Defence Procurement had once mentored Sarah during her brief stint as a junior analyst at GCHQ. They hadn't spoken in years.

But when the call came in *"urgent intelligence leak, national security, John Winters"*, Merrin had agreed to five minutes. Nothing more.

In the minister's office, Sarah placed the encrypted drive on the table between them.

"This is about Operation Glasshouse," she said. "It's real. It's in motion. The first drone strike is less than two hours out."

Merrin narrowed her eyes. "Where did you get this?"

Sarah leaned forward. "From John Winters' archive. And from someone codenamed Keyhole. He worked inside Helix. He was *there* at the beginning. He says John helped build the network."

The minister's brow furrowed. "John Winters was a traitor."

"No," Sarah said, her voice quiet. "He was *Kestrel at one point.* He ran it in the very earliest days. Then he tried to shut it down."

Ten minutes later, Alex was standing by the fence with hands raised and a loud, clear voice.

"I have a message for RAF Command. A strike is coming. Drones. Today. Internal compromise. You need to shut down uplinks and isolate your signal systems immediately."

Gasps. Phones came out. One man started filming.

Nikolai stood further back, pushing the warning through a local emergency frequency bouncing the signal directly to the base's civil-military liaison channel, using aviation metadata to camouflage the packet.

Within moments, base security began approaching fast.

A pair of armed police exited a nearby gate and headed straight for Alex, their radios crackling.

"Sir! On the ground, now!"

"I'm not a threat!" Alex shouted, kneeling as instructed. "I'm trying to *stop* one."

The sergeant who'd been chatting nearby had stepped aside, speaking urgently into a headset.

Behind the fence, someone was listening.

Inside the base, the emergency message flashed on Wing Commander Stuart Watkins terminal. The digital flag was embedded in an innocuous flight manifest request until the encryption unpacked itself.

DRONE STRIKE IMMINENT. INTERNAL SIGNAL BEACON ACTIVE. SLEEPER OPERATIVE CONFIRMED.
LOCATION: SOUTH UTILITY SHED. SOURCE: WINTERS, RED FLAG PROTOCOL.

The name *Winters* hit him like a hammer.

He knew that name. Everyone in his generation of Intelligence did.

Watkins slammed the lockdown alarm.

Outside, the base lights flickered and klaxons wailed.

The guards surrounding Alex froze mid-handcuff as sirens within the base erupted. One of them tapped an earpiece, confused, then stepped back.

"What the hell…"

From the far runway, a formation of F35s was ordered into immediate holding pattern. Vehicles rolled across the tarmac toward a small, unassuming maintenance block.

There buried inside a toolbox behind a locked utility panel security found a compact signal repeater pulsing faint green.

A rogue transmitter. Emitting encoded drone coordinates.

And beside it a body.

Callum Bryce.

Dead. Self-inflicted toxin.

A Russian Helix sleeper agent.

Thirty minutes later, Alex sat in the back of a base security vehicle, still handcuffed but no longer treated like a lunatic.

Nikolai paced outside, arms folded, silent as he watched helicopters circle overhead.

The crisis had been contained.

Just barely.

But they both knew what it meant.

Helix had infiltrated deeper than anyone imagined. And this… this was just the *first* firebreak.

Chapter 27: The Minister's Dilemma

Portcullis House, Westminster, the ceiling lights buzzed quietly overhead. Sarah Lane sat across from Minister Rachel Merrin, still in the same rumpled jacket from the early hours. Her fingers tapped restlessly against the flash drive on the desk between them. It contained not just Helix secrets but the counter-secrets. The names of Key Politicians. The sleeper agents. The trigger orders.

And buried deeper still: Kestrel's true identity.

Rachel Merrin studied her for a long moment.

"You expect me to believe John Winters built this… weaponised it… and then just had a change of heart?"

Sarah held her gaze. "No. I expect you to believe what's in the files. What the metadata proves. What the dead man at RAF Marham confirms. Winters tried to dismantle the machine from the inside."

Merrin folded her hands together. "Even if I believe you and I'm not saying I do, you're asking me to go public with intelligence that implicates members of our own national Government, even *two sitting NATO liaisons*. You know what that means?"

"Yes," Sarah replied quietly. "It means doing your job."

The minister stared at her, hard. Then slowly pushed her chair back.

"I'm going to need proof this wasn't planted by foreign actors. No red herrings. No 'unknown whistleblower.' I want the root certificate. The original system John used. Otherwise, I'll be treated as the fool who fell for a false flag."

Sarah slid another chip across the desk.

"The original architecture is on this. Direct from a vault in Zurich. The encryption keys were split between John's biometric and his sons. We've reconstructed the whole tree."

"And if I verify this…" Merrin asked slowly.

"Then you'll know this wasn't East vs. West," Sarah said. "It was *inside the house all along*."

Alex leaned back in the plastic chair, blood seeping through the fresh dressing on his arm. Across the table, Major Cullen, an RAF intelligence liaison, flipped through the fourth page of his notes with visible irritation.

"You accessed a protected signal band. You impersonated a flight operations control node. You activated a base-wide comms alarm under false credentials. And you expect me to believe *you're not a hostile actor?*"

Alex smiled faintly. "You shut the beacon down, didn't you?"

Cullen didn't answer.

"I'm not here to save face," Alex said. "I'm here because your systems were *compromised*. Your own man was running uplinks inside your airfield."

"Lieutenant Bryce is… under investigation," Cullen said tightly.

"He's dead."

Cullen froze.

Alex leaned forward. "Do the maths. What happens when the other bases light up? You think Marham was a one-off?"

Cullen looked at him for a long time then stood.

"You're free to go. But we'll be watching."

"Then watch carefully."

Outside RAF Marham, Nikolai stood by the edge of the car park, hands in the pockets of his coat, watching planes skim the clouds above the horizon.

Alex limped toward him, rubbing his sore arm. "Three hours of stonewalling and bad tea."

Nikolai grunted. "You hold up?"

"I said just enough to get out. Not enough to burn."

They climbed into the battered hatchback and Alex turned the ignition. "Where's Sarah now?"

Nikolai checked his phone. "Still inside Westminster."

"And the drive?"

"With her. But she won't hand it over."

Alex glanced at him.

"She's going to make them choose."

Westminster, Minister Merrin's Office the screen flickered once more as the final verification key unlocked.

Minister Merrin's hand slowly curled into a fist.

She tapped her intercom.

"Get me MI5. And close the door."

In a shadowed private room elsewhere in Westminster, a man in a tailored navy suit watched a secure monitor showing Sarah Lane's visit log.

He frowned.

Then made a single phone call.

"Activate *Protocol Blacklight.* They're getting too close."

Sarah Lane's instincts fired the moment minister Merrin stepped out to "brief the PM's security advisor." Something about the way Merrin avoided eye contact. The clipped tone. Too polite. Too rehearsed.

Sarah had trusted her once, but now, the walls felt tighter.

Still syncing the final logs from John's archive to the Zurich vault, Sarah pulled the drive early and pocketed it. She shut the laptop and slid it into her courier bag just as footsteps echoed in the corridor outside.

Not heels.

Boots. Heavy. Deliberate.

Her breath caught.

She didn't wait.

She slipped out the rear of the office, exiting through the adjoining hallway meant for cleaning staff, just seconds before the door burst open.

Three men entered.

Tactical suits. Earpieces. No badges.

One scanned the empty office and cursed under his breath.

Sarah was already gone vanishing into the labyrinth of Parliament before the kill order could find her.

Chapter 28: Shadows in the Rain

Manchester wasn't a safe haven. Not really. But after RAF Marham and the chaos in Westminster, it felt like the only place left where they might find room to breathe.

Alex, Nikolai, and Sarah met in a small apartment above a Turkish bakery in Rusholme. The smell of warm flatbreads and lamb drifted up from below, a strange comfort amid the tension. The rain tapped steadily against the windowpanes, the same familiar grey drizzle that had defined much of Alex's life here. But now, everything felt different.

Alex looked older than he had even a few weeks ago. His face was drawn, eyes shadowed by exhaustion, but beneath that weariness burned something harder. Determination. Nikolai had cleaned up as best he could, though the war still clung to him in invisible ways: a twitch of the eyes, a stiffness to the shoulders. Sarah, ever composed, paced like a caged animal, one hand constantly on her burner phone.

"London's compromised," she said, without preamble. "After Merrin turned, I don't trust anyone inside the Circle. Argus has deeper hooks than we thought."

Alex leaned forward. "So, what now? We just sit here and wait for them to find us?"

"No," Sarah said. "We start looking into your father's Manchester files. He knew something. Something he couldn't say out loud."

It began with the old laptop, its battered shell covered in faded MI6 asset tags. Alongside it: two USB sticks, an envelope of old photographs, and a list of locations with handwritten notes.

One name kept recurring: The Narrows.

Sarah cross-referenced the name and found it tied to an old garage on the edge of Cheetham Hill, near where canal locks fed into the old industrial estate. Local legend said the garage was used for stripping stolen cars. But John's files told a different story. It was a waypoint. A clearing house for something larger.

"John was tracking a drug-financing pipeline," Sarah explained, her eyes scanning the files. "From Pakistan. Through Turkey. Into Manchester. Look at this, he linked it to a shell company under a name tied to Argus: Vanguard Alchemy."

Alex recognised another name buried in the notes: Reece "Rhino" Ghaffer. A known enforcer from back in the day. Ex-boxer. Ran doors and debt collection within the Asian community, then graduated to high-stakes protection for wealthy clients. Rumour was, he was now Argus's man in the North.

That evening in Cheetham Hill, the clubs still pulsed with cheap lights and muffled basslines spilling from half-empty bars, but beneath it all, something darker hung in the air. Not just the cold. Control. Territory. Resource.

They found the garage nestled behind a crumbling warehouse tagged with gang graffiti and Arabic symbology, a hybrid that made Alex's stomach churn. They approached on foot, splitting up. Sarah kept lookout across the street with a burner phone pressed to her ear, pretending to argue in Romanian.

Inside the garage compound, the hum of machinery buzzed behind shuttered doors. A lone mechanic, early 30s, skinhead, dark beard, missing a tooth smoked near a half-gutted van. He barely glanced at them until Alex said the name "Merrin Holdings."

The man's face changed instantly. Fear. Recognition.

"We're not cops," Alex added calmly. "We just want to talk."

The mechanic led them to a backroom under the pretence of checking stock, an oil-stained corridor leading to a makeshift office lit by a halogen strip. The walls were papered with maps, delivery manifests, CCTV grids. A half-empty bottle of Serbian rakija sat next to a stack of phones.

They met Reece "Rhino" Ghaffer here, a barrel-chested Asian man with aggressive posture and dead eyes. He wore an old bomber jacket and sat behind the desk like a CEO of something far less legitimate.

"You've got five minutes," Rhino said without looking up.

Alex dropped a file on the desk. Inside: photographs of supply lines, crypto wallet keys, intercepted Argus emails. "We know what you're moving. And who you're working for."

Rhino's lips curled. "You lot don't know shit."

"We know enough," Sarah stepped in, voice sharp. "Enough to link Argus to Manchester's drug trade and associated arms supplies. Enough to know Helix was designed to expose the pipeline from warzones to UK cities."

Rhino leaned back slowly, sizing them up. Then he laughed, a sound that echoed off the metal walls like a warning.

"You think this is about drugs?" he sneered. "It's economics, love. Supply chains. The new currency's not cash, it's leverage. First weapons. Now food. Water. Energy. Control that, and you don't need armies. You own everything already."

Nikolai stepped forward, slow and cold. "Then consider this a disruption."

Before Rhino could respond, the lights in the garage flickered once, then cut out completely, plunging the room into sudden darkness. Sarah was already moving, her instincts razor-sharp. "We've got company," she muttered, drawing back from the desk.

They didn't hesitate. Alex shoved open the rear fire exit as the low growl of engines approached from the street outside. Two blacked-out SUVs rolled to a halt, their doors cracking open in near-silent synchrony.

Police?

Heavily built silhouettes emerged, tactical gear, close-shaven heads, rifles slung low. Para military in appearance, just like Rhino. Trained for violence, Bred for silence.

Alex and Nikolai disappeared into the alley's shadows without a word, Sarah right behind them. The Police hadn't seen them yet, but it wouldn't take long. The breach would be obvious.

Rhino's operation had been compromised.

Back at the flat

"You heard what he said?" Sarah asked, stripping off her jacket. "This is bigger than drugs. Argus is using the chaos from the war to build a new kind of empire. Warzone to street corner. Kalashnikovs to crack. But it doesn't end there."

She pulled a page from John's folder, highlighting a passage scrawled in red ink: *'Control the scarce, control the system. Food. Water. Movement.'*

"They're laying foundations for something post-collapse," she said. "When institutions fail, it won't be bombs that control people, it'll be bottled water and bread."

Alex stared at the Helix drive again. John's files weren't just a whistleblower cache. They were a roadmap, a war strategy. Expose the pipeline. Collapse the system. Clean house.

"But why Manchester?" Nikolai asked.

"Because it's a blind spot," Alex said. "Everyone's watching London. Here, they've had years to build in silence."

Sarah nodded, grim. "Helix wasn't just intelligence. It was an insurance policy. Your dad knew his death was inevitable. He just hoped we'd be smart enough to finish what he started."

Manchester was no longer a place to hide.

It was ground zero.

Chapter 29: Burned Bridges

The streets of Openshaw still shone with the memory of rain, slick tarmac glinting under sodium lights, the gutters humming with runoff. Manchester's cold had teeth this time of year, wet and invasive, seeping into bone.

Alex stood alone outside the old depot, its presence squatting behind high steel fencing like some dormant military relic. It had once been a logistics hub for the British Army, shuttling materiel to the frontlines of Afghanistan. Now it served a quieter war, a private security compound draped in the civilian skin of subcontracting.

He'd last seen Lou Donnelly in Helmand. Back then, Lou was all cracked knuckles and gallows wit, a logistics specialist who could conjure a generator or satellite dish out of dust. A fixer. Sharp. Useful. Dangerous in a way most supply officers weren't. He had connections in Karachi, Sofia, Lagos. If it moved, Lou could get it moving faster.

After the MOD cutbacks, Lou had drifted into the liminal world between contracting and something darker. Word, was he ran kit and arms for Argus in Eastern Europe. Then deeper still: crowd control, black-zone destabilisation, economic shaping.

Now, standing in the wind outside the repurposed compound, Alex knew this wasn't going to be a friendly reunion.

He stepped through the reinforced entryway and into the hard light of the depot's interior. It stank of oil, gun grease, and cold concrete. Security booths had been crammed inside converted cargo containers, the walls lined with monitors streaming thermal and aerial surveillance feeds. Tactical gear hung from open racks, plate carriers, encrypted comms, even ration packs stamped in Cyrillic.

Lou emerged from behind a mesh barrier, taller than Alex remembered. Broader too, with a thick beard, scarred jawline, and a tension in his frame that hadn't been there before. His eyes moved over Alex like a scanner.

"Alex fucking Winters," he muttered, arms crossed over a worn fleece. "Didn't think I'd see your face again. Thought you were out of the game."

"I was," Alex replied. "Then my old man handed me a data drive soaked in blood."

Lou smirked. "Still dramatic."

"I need to know what Argus is doing in Manchester. There's money moving, drugs, weapons. My dad was tracking it before they killed him."

Lou's eyes hardened. "Careful."

"I'm not here to play the tough guy," Alex said. "But I'm not leaving without answers."

For a long moment, Lou said nothing. Then he walked to a table and cracked open a bottle of filtered water. He drank slowly, then held it up, examining the label like it meant something.

"You ever think about why companies like this are buying up land near the Pennines?" he said flatly. "They're not planting crops, mate. They're bottling aquifers. Straight from the groundwater. Not for sale now, but for later. After the price goes up."

Alex frowned. "What the hell are you talking about?"

Lou turned, voice lower now. "You think this is about heroin or rifles? Those are old plays. What's coming next is control, real control. Water. Food. Clean air. You engineer scarcity, then you own demand. That's where the power lives."

Alex said nothing, his chest tightening.

Lou continued. "Create instability, push immigration flows, collapse old supply chains, weaponise inflation. The more pressure you create, the more control you gain. When twenty cities run dry, who do you think gets to choose who drinks first?"

"And Argus is doing this?" Alex asked, incredulous.

"Argus is just a brand," Lou shrugged. "The real operators? They wear suits and build tax shelters in Singapore. Helix isn't a leak, it's a roadmap. Supply the chaos. Own the solution."

Alex's fists clenched. "And the kids overdosing in Cheetham Hill? The housing blocks going dark because someone cuts the power. You justify all that because you're part of the 'solution'?"

Lou's jaw ticked. "Don't pretend like this is new. Governments have been doing it since Rome. You just don't like that it's local now."

Alex stepped forward. "You were a soldier. You knew right from wrong. What happened?"

Lou looked away. "I saw the game. And I learned how to win it."

They stared at each other. The silence between them was sharp enough to bleed.

"You think you're different?" Lou asked. "What are you gonna do, Alex? Publish a blog? Call a hotline? This system survives people like you."

Alex stepped back. "Maybe. But it burns every time it forgets people like me exist."

Lou didn't answer.

Alex turned on his heel and left the room, slamming the metal door behind him.

The wind outside had picked up. Harder now. Like something gathering.

He walked into it, hood up, the sound of sirens far off in the distance. The depot behind him loomed in the dark, silent and watching.

Now he understood.

Helix wasn't just about war.

It was a market.

A system of engineered dependency, chaos in one hand, contracts in the other. They didn't just profit from collapse. They planned it.

Water. Power. Food. Security.

The new commodities of control.

And Manchester wasn't a battlefield. It was a proving ground.

Chapter 30: Blood Money

The café on Oldham Street was all steamed windows and second-hand jazz, the kind of place built to look anonymous. Sarah sat near the back, laptop open, the Helix interface ghosted on her screen behind a local property site. Across from her, Nikolai scrolled through banking statements scraped from shell accounts, most flagged by John's old software as dormant or low risk.

Until now.

"Third time this week," Nikolai muttered, his finger tapping the screen. "Look, same holding account, different incoming source. One's a food distributor in Donetsk. One's a furniture shop in Stockport."

Sarah leaned closer. "And the recipient?"

"Hatherleigh Logistics Ltd. Based in Salford Quays. Supposed to be a bulk shipping firm, but there's no fleet registry. No personnel records. Just tax filings, neat and tidy."

She pulled up another file. "That company name appears three times in the Helix node cluster tagged *Black Signal*. Same cluster as Argus, Trident Group, and that fake NATO procurement front."

They looked at each other.

"It's not just drugs," Sarah said. "It's a financial arm. Smuggling routes. Laundering assets. This isn't local crime, it's infrastructure."

Just then, Sarah's phone buzzed. One word from Alex: "Confirmed."

They met an hour later in an abandoned car park beneath a tower block in Hulme. The rain had begun yet again, thin and icy.

"I just came from Lou," Alex said, voice low. "He's in deep. Argus are using gang-run logistics to shift product through the city. They don't need intelligence networks anymore; they've got supply chains. Real-time, dirty, and profitable."

Sarah frowned. "What kind of product?"

"Fentanyl. Weapons. Cash. Anything traceable gets scrubbed through Ukrainian shell companies, then re-emerges clean in Salford, Moss Side, or Cheetham Hill."

Nikolai stiffened. "I know that name, Hafez al-Masri. It came up on a donor list in Kyiv. Argus funnelled money through a so-called cultural exchange foundation tied to Beirut, but it was really al-Masri's network smuggling opiates out of Helmand through the Levant corridor and into Europe via North African ports."

Alex swore under his breath. "That's the connect. Argus funds the war, then launders the profits through the streets of the Uk through crime networks"

Sarah opened her laptop again, fingers flying. "This is how they stay invisible. They've mapped warzones to domestic economies. The city's gangs are just another division. Local enforcers. Local influence. Local silence."

They were silent for a beat.

Then Alex stepped forward. "We find the keystone. The person bridging both worlds Argus black ops and the Manchester underworld."

Sarah narrowed her eyes. "We take them down; we cut the pipeline."

"I'll talk to Jo Khan," Sarah said. "She still works within the National Crime Agency she'll know where the pressure points are."

Nikolai cracked his knuckles. "And if not... I know people who owe my father."

As they left the car park, a black motorbike idled across the street. The rider didn't move. Just watched. Then drove off.

Alex clocked it.

"They know we're back."

Chapter 31: Hunted Ground

Moss Side, once vibrant and defiant, now felt like part of a city caught between worlds, half-forgotten by redevelopment, half-owned by ghosts. The wind carried the faint scent of fried chicken, damp brick, and the tension of old grudges simmering under neon shopfronts.

Alex adjusted the collar of his coat as he and Nikolai walked along Claremont Road. His eyes scanned windows, alley mouths, rooftops. Nothing felt right. Too quiet. No kids out, no idle laughter, no scooters tearing up the side streets. Just silence and eyes.

"Still think this is worth it?" Nikolai muttered, hands deep in his hoodie pocket. His accent had softened, but his wariness was sharp as ever.

"Lou said he had something. Something he couldn't say over the phone." Alex didn't slow his stride. "But we treat this like a setup. Because it probably is."

Sarah's voice buzzed quietly in their earbuds. She was parked two blocks east in the battered red Golf, engine running, eyes on the rearview. "Nothing so far," she said. "But don't trust still water."

They rounded the corner near an old laundrette boarded up with police tape half-torn and sun-faded. That's when Alex saw it a flash of movement. Not clumsy enough for gang scouts. Too smooth. Professional.

"Six o'clock," Alex muttered.

Nikolai glanced in a shop window reflection. Two men, hoods low, walking just a bit too casually. A third stepped out from a kebab shop entrance, falling into line behind them.

"They're flanking us," Nikolai said. "Too tight for locals. These are trained."

"Argus," Alex growled. "They're using the gangs for cover."

The tension snapped as a fourth figure broke from the shadows across the road, heading straight for them. No time for doubt. Alex grabbed Nikolai's sleeve. "Run."

They cut left into an alley behind an abandoned community centre. The rain-slick brick walls closed in as they sprinted through puddles and rubbish bags, the sound of boots behind them. The chase was surgical, precise pressure on every exit. Argus wasn't just watching. They were herding.

A voice called from behind. "Winters! You want to die like your old man?"

Alex didn't look back. He vaulted a broken fence, Nikolai close behind. Another alley. Then another. Dead end.

"Shit," Nikolai hissed, spinning to face the approach. "Trapped."

The enforcers closed in. Five of them now. No visible weapons, but the way they moved said they didn't need them. One wore gloves. Not for warmth for grip. For violence.

Then screeching tyres. Headlights exploded around the corner.

Sarah's car burst into the alley with a howl of rubber and diesel. "Down!" she screamed.

The Golf slammed into one of the attackers, sending him flying. The others dove aside. In the confusion, Alex yanked Nikolai toward the car. They dove into the back seat as Sarah floored it in reverse, clipping another with the bumper as they roared back out onto the main road.

Bullets shattered the rear window, but they were gone.

Breathless. Alive.

In the backseat, Alex held his ribs, heart hammering. "Lou set us up."

"Or he's dead," Sarah said coldly, eyes scanning the mirror. "Either way, they're escalating."

Nikolai wiped blood from his temple. "They're not just cleaning up. They're hunting."

Alex nodded grimly. "And now they know we won't go quietly."

They vanished into the sprawl of South Manchester as the rain returned, heavier than before. The city was no longer just a battleground. It was a map of enemies hunting for them.

Chapter 32: Ghosts in the Bank

The street outside the credit union was deserted, the kind of silence that felt deliberate, like a stage cleared just before the curtain rises. Security shutters rattled in the wind, and the flicker of streetlights cast fractured shadows across the concrete. Everything about the building said "neglected finance co-op," but Alex knew better. This was ground zero.

Alex and Sarah, and Nikolai moved in silence, ducking through side alleys and shuttered walkways. Their destination was unassuming: a modest, grey-fronted credit union tucked between a vape shop and a boarded-up dentist's surgery. No signage. Just a laminated poster on the door offering *low-interest business loans* and *community support*. Grassroots finance. The kind of place that never drew suspicion and that made it perfect.

Sarah checked her phone. "We've got a six-minute window. Their systems run an automated maintenance update just before midnight. Firewalls drop. CCTV loops."

Alex nodded. "So we ghost in."

Nikolai stayed silent, his coat pulled tight. His nerves weren't from fear it was the feel of being on the edge again, walking the same war wire he'd lived on in Ukraine. But now, the enemy wasn't in uniform. It wore ties, moved money, and walked the halls of Parliament.

Sarah produced a chipped key card and swiped it. The glass door buzzed open.

Inside, the place was clinically sterile, cheap pine desks, grey carpet tiles, the hum of fluorescent lighting. But behind the bland facade was something else entirely.

Alex moved to the back office while Sarah slid behind the reception terminal, plugging in a flash drive loaded with Helix's access protocols. Within seconds, the system cracked open like a rotted vault door.

"I'm in," she whispered.

Nikolai stood watch at the front window, eyes scanning the quiet street. The tension was thick. Something about this job felt heavier.

Sarah's eyes darted across the screen. "Here it is. This place is just a front. It's been moving crypto, hard cash, and gold-bond wire transfers across at least three continents."

Alex leaned over her shoulder. The names of shell companies scrolled across the screen like a digital hitlist.

Mirado Assets AG – Liechtenstein
Eastern Passage Trading Co. – Georgia
Zayed Terra Limited – UAE

All squeaky clean on the surface. But dig deeper and the rot showed.

Sarah clicked into a flagged ledger, her voice tightening. "Look at the pattern. The transfers spike every time a major vote happens in Parliament. Every time there's an arms procurement bill. Every time a blackout hits a weapons shipment log. It's bribery. Sanctioned in code."

Then she stopped, frozen.

One name flashed across the screen: J. Merrin Holdings.

The same alias she'd seen in her files tied to corrupt MPs and Westminster lobby networks. The same shell John had circled in his handwritten notes months before his death.

Sarah swallowed hard. "He was onto it. All of it."

Alex exhaled slowly, the air thick with something heavier than revelation. "John was building a map. This… this was his cornerstone."

"Merrin Holdings is registered to an address in Dubai," she continued. "But it was originally set up in Gibraltar. No tax trace, no ownership trail. But Helix's metadata reveals a buried line item: John Winters. External Source. Field-Originated. 2021."

Nikolai turned from the window. "So they knew he had it."

Sarah nodded. "And they killed him before he could publish it and why he was so desperate to get Nikolia to safety."

Silence pressed in.

On the screen, more data unfolded. Offshore transfers disguised as charitable foundations. A fake shipping company routing heroin-laced fertilizer through Bulgaria. Aid trucks that never made it to Gaza. And all of it every wire, every crypto wallet somehow connected back to this small, forgotten building in Manchester.

"I've seen this before," Nikolai said. "Oligarch laundering systems. But this... it's hybrid. Government and gang. Intelligence and insurgent. No lines."

Sarah's fingers danced across the keys. "There's more here. Look, *resource flow modelling*. Water, grain, lithium, fertilizer. Supply simulations run by Argus through a proprietary platform called Aegis."

"Food and water," Alex said darkly. "Control the supply, you don't need armies. You dictate price, access... stability."

"They're not preparing for war," Sarah said. "They're preparing to profit from the collapse after it."

A short list. Handwritten. Five names, circled.

One of them: Merrin.

Another: Rhino Ghaffer.

And at the bottom, in a different pen... one word, underlined.

Kestrel.

Alex stared at it, the letters sharp and deliberate.

"Kestrel... Who is that?" he murmured.

Sarah didn't answer at first. "The name's appeared three times. Once in John's personal journal. Once in a restricted folder from Helix. And once here tied to a shell account routing payments to both Argus and an unnamed arm of the Foreign Office."

Nikolai frowned. "Could be a handle. Codename. Or...?"

"Or" Sarah said softly, "it's the architect behind all of this."

They stood there in the glow of the screen. Outside, the world passed by, unaware that something ancient, complex, and treacherous had slipped beneath its skin.

And somewhere out there, in the shadows of finance and war, Kestrel was still moving pieces across the board.

Outside, the street remained quiet. But the mood inside the credit union had shifted. The enemy wasn't at the gates. It was inside the vaults.

Nikolai stepped closer. "We need to copy everything. Helix isn't finished; it's just begun."

Sarah nodded and ran the extraction protocol. Files streamed onto the encrypted drive, 24%... 46%... 79%.

A sudden buzz.

"Contact on the alley," Nikolai said. "Two men. Civilian clothes. No movement pattern. But they're watching."

Sarah unplugged the drive at 91%. "Good enough."

They moved quickly, slipping out the rear exit through a fire door wedged open with a mop bucket. Sarah wiped the cameras as they left. No traces. No evidence.

Just ghosts in the bank.

Chapter 33: Redline

Friday night in Moss Side had a rhythm, not just the low basslines thudding from passing cars or the half-shouted conversations spilling out of fried chicken shops and betting parlours. It was the rhythm of a city straining under tension. Of territory patrolled, not policed. Where turf was negotiated in silence, eyes, nods, and phone calls and broken violently if the wrong line was crossed.

Alex had been gone from Manchester long enough to forget how close the edges always felt here. But tonight, walking through a narrowing street off Claremont Road with Nikolai and Sarah behind him, he could feel it. The city wasn't just restless it was volatile. Like something waiting to snap.

They passed a shuttered convenience store, its metal grille tagged with layered graffiti, old gang marks overwritten with new ones. Sarah clocked it too.

"These symbols aren't local," she murmured. "Eastern, Chechen or Albanian influence."

"Argus imports muscle," Alex said grimly. "They don't build it."

Sarah had pulled intel from a Helix archive node buried under a phoney NGO grant. It had flagged this street, not the houses themselves, but an old mechanics' yard repurposed for nighttime deliveries. The metadata suggested crypto wallets were being activated nearby in two-hour bursts, always tied to movement in and out of a single location.

Weapon stockpiles. Cash. Maybe encrypted comms kits.

They approached from the back, an alley hemmed in by garage walls and half-toppled fencing. Rubbish spilled from split bags. The smell of damp brick and poor drains clung to everything.

Sarah checked her phone. "Three pings on the wallet tracker. They're active now."

Alex slowed, raised a hand. They moved like a team again. No words needed. Nikolai looped around left. Sarah posted by a wall at the mouth of the alley, pretending to scroll on her phone. Alex pushed forward toward the old garage gate.

And then a sound. Low, subtle at first. Tyres, too fast. Brakes.

From the far end of the alley, a black BMW whipped around the corner, its headlights killing the darkness like a camera flash. The vehicle skidded to a halt, driver's side window down.

Alex caught the glint of metal.

Automatic fire erupted. Short bursts. Precision.

Bullets slammed into bins and brick, spraying splinters of red dust. Alex dropped flat, grabbing Nikolai by the collar and dragging him behind a stack of crates. Sarah dove behind a cement post, shielding herself with an overflowing recycling bin.

Alex's ears rang. Concrete chipped near his feet.

These weren't street gang tactics. No shouting. No panicked movement. Just swift, coordinated fire.

"This isn't gangland," Alex hissed. "These are trained operators."

Nikolai nodded, grim. "Same cadence. Same weapons. Same loadouts I saw in Donetsk."

One of the shooters stepped out from the BMW balaclava, grey tactical jacket, ear-piece. He raised a submachine gun and advanced.

Alex scanned fast. He had no firearm, not in Britain. But he still had reflexes.

He grabbed a loose scaffold bar from behind the crates and waited, crouched low. The shooter stepped around the corner too fast.

Alex exploded upward, slamming the bar across the man's wrist with a sickening crunch. The weapon clattered to the ground. Nikolai lunged forward, punching him square in the throat. The man dropped without a sound.

Another shot cracked, this time from further down the alley. Not aimed. Suppressive.

A second man advanced more cautious.

Sarah shouted from across the street, drawing attention. "Police!" she yelled. "I'm calling them now!"

The man froze. Tactical hesitation. British streets weren't Afghanistan, noise mattered.

Alex grabbed the submachine gun from the fallen man and aimed at the ground near the advancing shooter.

One shot. Deliberate.

A warning.

The shooter hesitated then turned and sprinted back to the BMW. Tyres screeched again. The vehicle peeled off, disappearing into the night.

Silence.

And then, a sound that chilled them more than gunfire.

A low, rattling breath.

They turned.

A teenager lay behind a bin across the alley, caught in the crossfire. He had been trying to run to escape the mayhem he had innocently been caught in. A pool of blood spread beneath him, soaking into a backpack.

Nikolai dropped to his knees beside him, checking his pulse. His face was pale, trembling.

"His name's Yusuf," he whispered, pulling a school ID from the jacket pocket. "He's thirteen."

Alex stood frozen. The street around them was still again but not quiet. Sirens wailed somewhere far off. Neighbours peeked through curtains. Nobody stepped outside.

Sarah moved slowly toward them, eyes wet, her voice low. "The shipment Nikolai tracked from Odessa it's here. I just confirmed it. Argus hardware. This wasn't a one-off."

Alex didn't answer.

He looked down the alley again. At the blood, at the bin riddled with bullet holes, at the cheap corner shop's smashed window reflecting red and blue lights in the distance.

They weren't just witnesses anymore.

They weren't just uncovering something.

This was real. The line had been crossed. And it was war.

Alex knelt beside Nikolai and closed the boy's eyes gently.

"Come on we need to go," he said, voice hoarse.

Chapter 34: House of Silence

The next morning, the city had moved on as it always did.

But something about Moss Side had shifted. Quiet wasn't peace here; it was recoil. The kind of silence that follows after someone's pulled a trigger and left the scene. Windows that once played music stayed closed. No kids on the corners. Just the slow hum of buses and the rattling nerves of a neighbourhood that had seen too much.

Alex didn't sleep.

He'd spent the night staring at John's encrypted files again. Rewatching footage from Odessa. Studying heat maps that cross-referenced crypto wallets, phone metadata, and financial laundering patterns across Greater Manchester.

One address had been pinged three separate times in the last 24 hours by an inactive wallet connected to J. Merrin Holdings a name Sarah had traced back to several offshore shell companies in Liechtenstein and the UAE.

A private financial cooperative on the edge of Chorlton's neat exterior, frosted windows, and signage that claimed to offer "community microloans." But behind that, a strange flurry of electronic activity. Wire transfers. Smart contracts. Crypto bridges connected to Georgian exchange nodes.

John had been tracking this place. He just never got the chance to walk through the door.

Now, it was their turn.

They arrived just before midday. A small sign above the door read: *Briarside Mutual Trust*. It looked like it hadn't changed since the early 1990s.

"Run quiet," Sarah murmured, adjusting her scarf and tucking a burner phone into her coat sleeve. "No sudden moves. We're clients. We're curious. Nothing more."

Alex nodded. Nikolai was already casing the CCTV placements above the door and rear alley. "They've got IR sensors. Movement triggers in both directions. These aren't standard for a credit union."

"They're watching for who *leaves*, not who enters," Sarah muttered. "That tells us something."

Inside, it smelled like carpet cleaner and old photocopier ink. An Asian woman at the desk mid-fifties, reading glasses, polite smile looked up from her terminal.

"Looking to open an account?" she asked.

"Something like that," Sarah said. "We've got an inheritance to move. Small trust. Based overseas."

The woman's smile barely faltered. "What country?"

"Lichtenstein," Sarah answered, just to see the flicker.

There it was a pause in the eyes. A soft intake of breath. A slight tap on the keyboard.

"I'll get the manager. He deals with foreign instruments," the woman said calmly, standing.

They were left alone for ninety seconds.

That was enough.

Nikolai glanced at the back room. "That desk lamp isn't on. But the shadows on the glass say someone's moving in there."

"Two phones inside the drawer," Alex added. "One flashing light."

Sarah pulled a small pen device from her coat and clicked it once. It vibrated. "Signal pinged. There's a blockchain validation key stored here. That wallet's active. It just processed a smart contract from *Zeyad Exchange* a crypto outlet in Dubai."

She turned slowly, eyes scanning the walls. "They're not laundering cash. They're moving value. In bulk. Borderless. Invisible."

Footsteps approached. A man entered the lobby.

Tall. Thin. Impeccably dressed in a tailored navy suit that didn't belong in a dusty Chorlton office. His hair was too neat, his cufflinks too polished. But the giveaway was the walk measured, balanced, coiled like someone who'd trained for decades to never look startled.

"Can I help you?" the man asked. His accent was British, but flattened boarding school, then intelligence training.

"Just here to move some assets," Alex said. "Quick in, quick out."

The man's smile didn't reach his eyes.

"Some things are easier moved than others," he said. "Names are sticky. History clings."

Sarah stepped forward. "We're not here for trouble. We just want to know what Merrin Holdings really is."

The man didn't blink. But the room shifted.

"You should leave," he said quietly. "You're already past the line."

Nikolai stepped forward, voice even. "You work for Kestrel?"

The name landed like a dropped stone.

The man said nothing, but his knuckles flexed slightly.

"That's what this is, isn't it?" Nikolai went on. "Helix wasn't just about drones or drugs or crypto. It's about architecture. Financial, digital, logistical. And it needs a conductor. A ghost to make it all move."

"You're talking in riddles," the man said. "Maybe you've been reading too much Cold War fiction."

Sarah stared at him, eyes narrowing. "Then why are you afraid to say who's behind the shell companies?"

Outside, a car pulled up silver estate, windows tinted.

The man's expression changed for the first time. "You should leave," he said again. "There are mechanisms in place. You don't want to trigger them."

Alex met his eyes. "John Winters died for this. We won't."

And then they left.

No alarms. No guns. Just silence.

But they all knew what that meant.

Back at the flat, the Helix map bloomed across the laptop screen.

Every link from Odessa to Moss Side, from crypto trades in Tbilisi to microloans in Chorlton fed into the same node.

Kestrel.

A code name, a call sign, maybe a person. Always upstream. Always one step removed.

Sarah zoomed in on the Briarside Mutual office, its tiny data footprint marked with a yellow triangle.

"Whoever they are," she said, "they're the architect of this entire structure."

Alex nodded slowly. "And if they know we're this close…"

Nikolai finished the thought: "Then we've already pulled the pin."

Outside, the silence grew heavy again.

But they weren't turning back.

Not now.

Not when they were this close to the truth.

Chapter 35: The Shadow Script

The upstairs apartment hummed with heat from the bakery ovens below, but none of them noticed. The three of them Alex, Sarah, Nikolai sat in the half-light, circled by screens, printouts, and handwritten notes from John's old Helix cache.

The name kept surfacing: Kestrel.

Not in a subject line. Never in sender fields. But embedded deep in metadata timestamps, cryptographic markers, filenames with feathered suffixes. Always just far enough out of reach. Like bait. Or a warning.

Alex paced. "Who the hell is this?"

Sarah didn't look up from her laptop. "Whoever they are, they don't exist in the open. Kestrel's not a codename it's a firewall. One that spans departments and overrides standard classification."

Nikolai nodded toward the decryption running on a second laptop. "This isn't a ghost," he muttered. "It's an architect."

The data led them into strange places. One file, *AssetControl_V3-K*, referenced a quiet, underfunded water purification contract in North Yorkshire buried beneath eight layers of shell companies, tied to the same grant system John had flagged.

Another flagged a policy memo with no author, dated March 2020:

"Strategic chokepoints are no longer kinetic. Water control is food control. Population pressure is leverage. Manufacture scarcity, and you write the rules."

Sarah read it aloud. No one spoke when she finished.

"Jesus Christ," Alex whispered. "This isn't about weapons."

"It never was," she replied. "This is about *control.*"

She clicked open another document internal comms logs flagged "FOR MOD/OSD/CO USE ONLY." The message stream referenced medicine diversion, infrastructure tenders, and transit hubs not in foreign war zones, but Leeds, Bristol, Manchester.

Control wasn't coming by force.

It would come through shortage. Dependency. Through need.

"Here," Nikolai said suddenly. He turned his screen. "A flagged source file 'Room 17b, Vauxhall Cross.' May 2024. Declassified audio."

Sarah played it. A distorted voice, male, careful with every word:

"Kestrel doesn't command. They curate. Pressure is applied through infrastructure, not ideology. Urban districts and councils restructured. Supply corridors re-prioritised. You starve a district not of food, but opportunity. Then offer relief. The grateful don't rebel."

Alex felt cold despite the warmth of the bakery.

Sarah whispered, "How many times has this been trialled? How many socially deprived towns, how many countries?"

They were silent for a moment.

Then Sarah leaned back in her chair. "I've worked inside these systems. MI5, Home Office, counter-extremism task forces. You think it's chaos at the top, but it's not. It's theatre. The real decisions are made in the margins by people like Kestrel. People you never see."

Nikolai looked up. "So why hasn't anyone stopped it?"

Sarah hesitated. Then: "Because too many benefit. Or they're afraid to speak out or challenge. Or they think it's necessary."

"That's the scariest part," Alex said. "They might think they're saving the country."

Later, Alex stood alone at the window, city lights flickering across the glass.

"John knew," he said. "That's why he vanished. That's why he left this for us."

He didn't look at Sarah when he asked, "You still believe in the system?"

Her answer took a beat.

"I believe in what it *could* be. But this?" She glanced down at the Helix drive. "This is rot. It's the kind of power that never asks permission, and never says sorry."

Alex nodded. The son of a spymaster. A soldier. A recovering addict trying to make sense of his father's war, a war he'd inherited without warning, or choice.

Kestrel wasn't just a name in the files.

It was the knife in the back of democracy.

And John had tried to stop it.

Sarah pulled a final document from the printer tray, a scanned letter, unsigned, no letterhead. Dated February 2025. Titled only:

Proposal: Civil Stress Modelling — Post-Resource Collapse

It spoke of coordinated water rationing trials. Temporary medicine shortages. Urban stress testing through energy access disruption. The targets weren't enemies abroad.

They were inner-city councils in Britain.

Sarah folded the page, hands trembling slightly. "We're not hunting criminals anymore. We're hunting planners."

Outside, the hum of late-night Manchester life continued, kebab vans, sirens, motorbikes pulling wheelies on Deansgate.

But inside that room, something shifted.
Trust in institutions.
In memory.
In blood.
And in the shadows, Kestrel watched.
Not from Moscow.
Not from Kabul.
But from inside the system.

Chapter 36: The Archive Leak

The air inside the flat was stifling. Not hot, just heavy. Like it carried weight. Like it had heard too much.

A second-hand fan wheezed in the corner but did nothing to cut through the silence.

Sarah sat hunched over her laptop, fingers moving through code with the kind of speed that only came with muscle memory and adrenaline. The glow from the screen cast ghost-light across her face, making the lines around her eyes sharper, older. A box of printed Helix data packets lay scattered on the floor beside her weeks' worth of decrypts and guesswork.

Nikolai paced near the window. His frame was restless, like a dog too long in a cage. He tugged back the curtain every thirty seconds to check the street below. He trusted nothing now, not the quiet, not the dark, not even the streetlights that flickered like faulty memories.

Alex leaned against the far wall, arms folded. Watching. Not Sarah. The screen. Waiting for something to appear.

And then it did.

A line of red across the terminal. A single flagged batch buried inside archived metadata from a Helix server node in Varna.

>> Archive Node: BRK/Helix-LN-FWD
>> Personnel Reference — Internal (Redacted/Restricted)
>> Parsing Alias Index…

There it was.

Codename: SHADOW INTERFACE
Alias: Lane, Sarah
Designation: Compliance Liaison – London Forward Team
Initiated: October 2017

Status: Flagged (Insubordinate — Do Not Reactivate)
Override Clearance: J. Winters – Non-DCL

The screen didn't flicker. But something else did.

Nikolai stopped pacing. His breath caught.

Alex stepped forward, eyes locked on the data like it was about to vanish.

"Tell me," he said quietly, "that's not you."

Sarah didn't answer right away. She was frozen. The air around her seemed to press in.

"It's not what it looks like," she said finally. Her voice had changed. Lower. Tighter. Defensive, but not panicked.

Alex didn't blink. "It looks like you were working for them."

Nikolai's fists clenched, arms rigid. "We trusted you."

"I never worked for Argus," Sarah snapped, spinning her chair around. "Not like that."

"Then what *is* it?" Alex asked.

She stood up, pushing the laptop away. "John embedded me. He recruited me as a quiet contact. Surveillance, he said. Forward-post monitoring. I passed information upstream, flagged anomalies, watched chatter between shell accounts and known assets. But he never told me the real structure."

"You were in their system," Nikolai said. "You were *named*. That's not casual."

Sarah stepped closer. Her hands weren't shaking, but her voice nearly cracked. "I was a pawn. Just like the rest of you. When I figured out who was really behind the funding trail... when I saw the names, the connections, they cut me off. Burned me. I couldn't go to MI5. Everyone was compromised or quiet. So, I disappeared."

"You disappeared," Alex repeated. "Right into our operation."

Her eyes narrowed. "You think I planned this? I found your father's drop box because I was looking for leverage. Something to protect myself. And I stayed because I realised what this really was."

"Did you?" Nikolai asked coldly. "Or are you still playing your part?"

The silence thickened. Alex looked between them. He wanted to believe her. He needed to. But trust, once cracked, didn't just glue itself back together.

Sarah finally exhaled. "Look at the rest of the file."

Alex turned back to the screen.

Status: Terminated. Ghost Protocol.
Reason: Suspected breach via Winters (John). Watch status activated.

"They marked me rogue," Sarah said. "Because John lied to me too. He was the only one who knew the scope. And the moment he vanished, so did my protection."

Nikolai didn't reply. He just stepped away from the window and dropped into a chair. His knuckles were white.

Alex stared at the screen. Everything about it made him sick not because it was unexpected, but because deep down, he'd feared something like this since the day they first met her.

But what mattered now was what *they* did with the truth.

"This changes things," Nikolai said eventually.

"Yeah," Alex muttered. "It does."

They both looked at Sarah.

"I'm not the enemy," she said. "I'm just what your father left behind."

No one spoke. Trust, that invisible tether frayed between them.

Outside, the city slept. But inside, three lives hung suspended over a fault line. And under pressure, fractures don't just crack, they split wide open.

Chapter 37: The Unseen Hand

The narrow hallway in the old records wing of Manchester's disused central telecom exchange smelled of dust and mildew but it was secure, off-grid, and unlisted. Beneath the forgotten data cables and rusting server panels, the last physical trace of MI5's Northern Archive still existed.

They'd tracked the lead to James Lawton, an ageing data analyst and former MI5 technical adviser. The kind of man who had known too much, kept his mouth shut for too long, and retired early after a "restructuring" swept through internal security in 2023.

Now he lived like a ghost, buried under redundancy pay and bitterness.

"He won't talk to anyone still drawing a government pension," Sarah warned. "He thinks everyone's tainted."

"Then it's good none of us are on payroll," Alex muttered, knocking on the steel door.

It opened three seconds later not wide, just enough for a cautious eye to peek through.

"Sarah Lane," said a quiet voice. "I should slam this shut."

"I'm not here for apologies, James," she said calmly. "I'm here because someone's rewriting history. And I think you know how dangerous that can be."

Another beat. Then the door creaked open.

Inside, the space looked like an analogue war bunker, maps pinned with string, boxes labelled by hand, a network of disconnected hard drives on steel shelves. A terminal hummed faintly in the corner, surrounded by old files stacked like a barricade.

James Lawton looked as though time had buried him halfway, faded jumper, grey stubble, thick glasses slipping down his nose. He didn't shake hands.

"You brought company," he said, eyeing Alex and Nikolai.

"They don't trust me," Sarah replied. "Not after the archive leak."

Lawton sighed. "Then I suppose I owe you some context."

He moved slowly to his desk, rifling through an envelope marked "LS2023 - Field Liaison, Non-Operational". Inside were old personnel notes, redacted performance reviews, and one internal memo that made Nikolai inhale sharply.

"Operative: LANE, SARAH — flagged for overreach in Operation SHARD-BRIDGE. Subject attempted to elevate risk assessments and notify ministerial oversight. Reprimanded for procedural breach. Clearance downgraded. Assignment terminated under Directional Authority: KESTREL."

Alex read it twice.

"You tried to warn them," he said slowly.

Sarah nodded. "I sent four flagged reports through John's back-channel. I called a real-time meeting with Domestic Oversight. Kestrel shut it down in less than 48 hours."

Lawton rubbed his temples. "You were lucky they didn't erase your career outright."

"They did," she said flatly. "I was reassigned, denied field access, then looped out of internal comms altogether. They put a red stamp on my record that said 'non-cooperative tendencies.' That was my professional obituary."

"And Kestrel?" Nikolai asked. "Who *is* he?"

Lawton looked at them. His eyes were tired, but something sharp flickered behind them fear, maybe. Or just the weight of too much knowledge.

"I don't know," he said carefully. "And that's the problem. I know every senior position in that structure from the last twenty years. There's no personnel match, no entry trace, no file chain. Kestrel is either a ghost, or someone with the authority to overwrite their own existence."

"So a top-level asset?" Alex asked. "Politician? Military?"

"Or worse," Lawton murmured. "Someone *between*. Someone who makes sure nothing ever makes it to daylight."

Silence fell over the room.

Sarah stepped away, looking at the documents strewn across the desk. She picked up a printed incident report one she'd filed in 2023 marked with an internal code and the words: *"Not actionable. Archive."*

"I gave them everything," she whispered. "And they filed it in a drawer."

Nikolai glanced at Alex, then back at her.

"You tried," he said quietly. "They punished you for it."

Alex's jaw clenched, but he nodded too. "It's not on you anymore."

Sarah turned, meeting both their eyes. "It *is* on me. I helped build the foundation Argus is using now even if I didn't know it at the time. So I'll help finish it."

Alex exhaled. The last of his doubt slipped away.

Lawton held out one more file a short transfer log from a month before John's death.

To: KESTREL – URGENT ENCRYPTED DROP

Subject: Winters Drive (Partial Contents)
Note: Helix is operational. Awaiting instructions.

"That's the signal," Lawton said. "That's when John knew they were onto him."

Nikolai stepped forward. "Then it's not just Helix anymore."

"No," Sarah said. "Now it's about exposure. And vengeance."

They walked out of the telecom bunker into the late afternoon haze, minds sharp, hearts steadier. For the first time in weeks, the lines were clear again.

Helix wasn't just a war file. It was a map of corruption and the names they were about to expose weren't just military. They were political. Economic. Institutional.

And somewhere in that tangle of power and silence, *Kestrel* was waiting.

Chapter 38: The Voice Behind the Curtain

The back of the former Openshaw logistics depot was silent now. The security lights had been cut. The CCTV towers loomed like dead cranes over the rain-scuffed gravel lot. Alex stood with his collar up, breath misting. It was cold but not just from the air.

Lou Donnelly had called him back. No excuses. No riddles.

Just: "Come alone. No guns. It's time."

Alex didn't trust it.

But he went anyway.

Inside, Lou's office hadn't changed. Tactical gear still lined the walls. Old maps. Flight manifests. A half-empty bottle of Polish vodka sat beside a cracked mug of instant coffee. Lou stood near the centre, his usual swagger dulled.

He looked worn, not tired, but bruised. Internally.

"You're late," Lou said.

"I didn't realise we were on the clock," Alex replied.

Lou exhaled through his nose, rubbing the bridge of his nose. "You ever feel like you're ten steps into something and just now realising it's a maze?"

"I'm living it," Alex said.

Lou walked over to the whiteboard. It had been wiped clean except for one name, written in red Sharpie.

KESTREL

He tapped it once. "They got to me."

Alex's stomach dropped.

"They threatened you?"

"Didn't have to," Lou said, sitting on the edge of the desk. "They offered me a contract extension. Double what I make now. Overseas jurisdiction. And immunity."

"For what?" Alex asked.

"For delivering you," Lou said. "And walking away clean."

Alex didn't move. "And?"

Lou stared at him for a long moment. "I've done a lot of shitty things, Winters. Some for the right reasons. Some for money. But handing you over to people like that? That ain't in my blood."

He reached behind the desk and slid over a hard drive. "Encrypted comms packet. You need to hear what they sent me."

Alex plugged it into his phone and let the file load. A moment later, the screen flickered, just a black screen, a waveform bar, and a voice that felt like cold glass.

Digitally masked. Genderless. Intonation warped. Calm, but surgical.

"We are aware of your investigation. We are aware of Helix. Of Winters. Lane. Nikolai. You're chasing ghosts built for your distraction. There is no single Kestrel. There is only the flight pattern. The system. The balance."

"This is your only offer. Walk away. Leave the Helix Drive where it is. Forget Merrin. Forget Argus. You will not be harmed. You will not be followed. Immunity, digital and physical, is guaranteed."

"Choose war, and you disappear. Like your father."

The audio cut. The screen faded to static.

Neither of them spoke for a moment.

Alex's pulse thudded in his ears.

"So," Lou said finally. "Still think this is about MPs and dirty money?"

Alex shook his head slowly. "This is deeper. This isn't just corruption. It's structure. It's the bones under the house."

Lou looked at him. "You still going to run at it head-first?"

"I don't run," Alex said. "And if we're being offered immunity, it means they're afraid. That means we're close."

Lou leaned back, rubbing the back of his neck. "You should know… some of the shipments we moved last year? Food security units. High-density water filtration tech. Controlled release meds. I didn't ask questions at the time. Just moved the crates. Now I'm thinking it wasn't for disaster zones."

"Population pressure," Alex said quietly. "Create demand by creating scarcity. Food, water, medicine. And they control the tap."

"War isn't the goal," Lou muttered. "It's the pressure cooker. The chaos lets them restructure."

Alex stepped back from the desk, jaw tight. "And Kestrel's the architect."

"No," Lou said. "Kestrel's the blueprint."

The two men stared at each other for a long moment then Alex picked up the drive.

"I'll need your help."

Lou nodded slowly. "I figured."

Outside, the wind shifted, sharp, metallic, carried over from the dead rails that cut through East Manchester. A city under siege not from bombs, but from silence. Supply chains. Fear.

As Alex stepped into the cold, a message pinged his phone from Sarah.

New trace. Financial records. Manchester shell. "Wingcliff Systems."
Owner unknown. Tied to Kestrel.

He texted back: "We move tomorrow. No more waiting."

Chapter 39: Pressure Points

The depot looked dead. Half its windows were broken, the gates rusted over with ivy and bad secrets. A storm hadn't rolled in, but the air was heavy, the kind that made skin itch and metal doors sweat.

Nikolai checked the rear approach again. "We're clear."

Sarah glanced at the signage barely visible under grime: Northstream Holdings - Authorized Personnel Only.

"Northstream," she murmured. "Same shell company that handled rations for the refugee camps in places like Iraq, Turkey, Syria and Gaza."

"And water tankers in Tbilisi," Nikolai added. "Both had outbreaks days after withdrawal."

She looked at him. "You think that was deliberate?"

"I think accidents don't usually come with supply chain redundancies built in," he replied. "Someone wanted chaos, then offered the cure."

Inside, the place smelled like dust and detergent. Overhead lights flickered, powered by a generator somewhere humming low behind walls. Sarah's boots echoed on concrete.

They came across the first stack of crates by a shuttered loading bay. Labels read in coded supply terms, but the Helix tagging system helped them decode it fast: *High-calorie food rations, Mobile desalination packs, Crisis-grade electrolyte boosters.*

She crouched, pulling a label closer into the light. "These aren't for relief. They're for control."

Nikolai said nothing. Just stared at the crates.

Then: "There's more in the back," he muttered.

They moved through a corridor lined with crates stacked like coffins, until they reached a reinforced door.

Sarah produced a crowbar from her satchel and worked the latch. It gave way with a groan.

Inside was colder, better sealed. Fluorescent lights clicked on revealing floor-to-ceiling pallets of high-efficiency water filtration units, climate-tolerant seed vaults, and digital ration lockers.

Each locker had biometric readers, already programmed for ID access.

Sarah stepped forward slowly, staring at the lineup of sealed boxes like they were body bags.

"They're building a dependency system," she said. "Access controlled by identity. Biometric rationing. In a full-blown crisis, they won't need armed men just access codes and food schedules."

Nikolai rubbed the back of his neck, processing. "This isn't even a worst-case prep. This is rollout-ready."

She turned. "Why Manchester?"

He shrugged. "Quiet supply routes. Minimal scrutiny. And a population dense enough to model behaviour across lines race, class, income, trust. Manchester's a testbed."

Sarah crouched by one locker, studying its interface. "Argus didn't just want control. They wanted predictive obedience. Push a community to the brink, offer controlled survival and you own the next decade of politics."

A long silence followed. Then Nikolai spoke carefully, like stepping across a frozen lake.

"I owe you an apology."

She didn't answer.

"I doubted you. After the Archive leak… I thought maybe you'd flipped. Maybe John wasn't the only one keeping secrets."

Still silence.

He pushed on. "You were right to be angry."

Sarah finally looked up, her expression unreadable. "You think that was anger? Try betrayal. You and Alex froze me out."

"I didn't know who to trust," Nikolai said.

She stood, slowly. "Then maybe you never trusted me in the first place."

"I did," he said. "And that's what scared me."

Another silence. He ran a hand through his hair, bracing.

"There's something else," he said. "Something I never told anyone, not even Alex."

She waited.

"When I was younger," he began, "I was approached by Russian intelligence. GRU. I was just starting work. They knew about my father John. Said he was a traitor. Said I could restore my family's honour. All I had to do was track his movements."

Sarah's eyes didn't move.

"I never took the deal. But I kept the contact number for months. Just in case."

"And did your father know?"

"I don't think so.

Sarah exhaled slowly, then turned to one of the sealed seed containers. "So you and I aren't so different. Recruited by someone we thought we understood. Burned when the truth got too complicated."

He nodded. "I didn't betray him. But I didn't prove him wrong, either."

"Legacy," she said bitterly. "It sticks like blood."

They stood for a while in the silence, surrounded by the quiet threat of engineered control. Crates filled with survival tech, just waiting for the collapse to come.

Sarah moved toward the far wall, where a series of whiteboards had been scrubbed half-clean. She sprayed light from her phone across one and saw faint markings still etched in marker.

"Phase Three – Northern Uplinks (UK Only)."
"Model Behaviour: 72-Hour Dependency Cycle."
"Water Access = Loyalty Tiers."

Sarah's voice was almost a whisper. "They're not just planning for a crisis. They're planning to *grade* us during it."

Nikolai tapped the biometric reader on the ration locker. "Control through scarcity."

She nodded. "And obedience through the illusion of choice."

Just then, Sarah's phone buzzed with a secure pulse message.

"Wingcliff Systems. 0600. Final breach protocol in play. Kestrel will know."

Nikolai raised an eyebrow. "Kestrel again."

Sarah's jaw tightened. "They're the axis. Everything turns on them. Or it."

As they exited the depot, Nikolai paused one last time and looked back at the stacked resources, not weapons, not cash but what people actually kill for when systems fall.

"Power used to come from fear," he said. "Now it comes from *need*."

Sarah met his eyes.

Chapter 40: Wingcliff Breach

The sun had not yet risen over the industrial horizon. Manchester lay wrapped in a heavy pre-dawn stillness a city caught in the hush before something breaks. Beneath that silence, Wingcliff Systems loomed at the edge of Trafford Park like a fortress draped in modern gloss: mirrored glass, biometric checkpoints, security drones that whirred overhead with surgical indifference.

Alex adjusted his collar beneath the hi-vis jacket he'd lifted from a delivery van an hour earlier. Beside him, Sarah keyed in an access sequence she'd stolen from a compromised Helix node. Nikolai waited in the rear, watching their flank, an earpiece crackling softly in his ear.

"Fourth floor. Sub server wing," Sarah muttered. "That's where the backups live. We hit the mirrors, copy the files, and ghost the system."

Alex gave a single nod. "We're in and out in twenty."

No one needed to say what they all felt. If this failed, there would be no retry. Wingcliff wasn't just a holding node for Argus's encrypted financials it was the *vault*. The heartbeat of supply-chain command. If what John had suspected was true, this place wasn't just a data farm.

It was where Kestrel watched the world.

They passed the first two security layers under the guise of maintenance subcontractors forged credentials, stolen tags. A security guard glanced at Sarah's ID but didn't linger. No one asked about the third person. Hi viz made people invisible.

The server wing was quiet, artificially chilled, and bathed in sterile blue-white light. Machines hummed like something breathing.

"This is it," Sarah said, stepping up to a fingerprint scanner. "Hold tight."

Behind her, Nikolai scanned the corridors. "No movement. Yet."

Sarah tapped through the admin override. The lock clicked.

They were inside.

Rows of stacked server columns rose like pillars in a cathedral of code. Red and green indicator lights pulsed softly like heartbeat monitors.

Alex approached the central rack. "This one. Tagged *BRI-VI*. British Infrastructure. That's the allocation we've been chasing since Ukraine."

Sarah plugged in a pocket drive. "Decrypting mirror cache. Keep watch. This'll take ninety seconds."

Nikolai moved toward the corner of the room, where a glass pane looked out into the corridor beyond.

He froze.

"Movement. South hall. Two figures. Tactical posture."

Alex cursed under his breath. "We're made."

Sarah didn't look up. "Thirty seconds."

The door behind them was reinforced. No way to block it for long.

Then Alex's phone buzzed, just once.

Lou Donnelly – Missed Call.

It was followed by a second message.

"Too late. I tried."

Alex's gut turned.

Nikolai caught it too. "Lou?"

Alex's voice was low, even. "We just got his goodbye."

Earlier that night, Salford Docks

Lou Donnelly sat alone in the back of a shipping container office, the lights low, a cup of cold coffee trembling in his hand.

He'd done it.

After two decades of grey ops, side deals, and logistics no one wanted to talk about, Lou had finally stepped off the path. He'd sent Alex everything copies of manifests, shipping routes, the Wingcliff schema.

Burned his clearance.

He'd walked outside, breathing the chemical-soaked air off the water like it might absolve him.

The silence was broken by a low hum. Not from a phone. From the drone.

It dropped just above head height sleek, matte black, no wider than a pizza box.

Lou turned, blinking into its red light.

The round hit him square in the chest.

No ceremony. No chance to explain.

Just a short, brutal sound *pfft* like someone flicking a towel.

He dropped. The drone hovered a moment, scanning for confirmation, then rose into the dark.

Lou Donnelly was gone.

And with him, the last man willing to name Kestrel aloud.

Back at Wingcliff

Something shifted in the air.

Alex's instincts kicked in before his brain did. He shoved Sarah sideways behind the server rack. "Move. Quiet. Now."

Nikolai slid back toward the corner of the room just as the server room door burst open. Two figures in black tactical gear stepped in smooth, efficient, silent. Not police. Not security.

Argus.

They didn't speak. One swept the room with a stun baton; the other went straight for the terminal. Clean-up crew.

Alex stepped out from behind a column like a shadow and caught the first man off-guard. He drove an elbow hard into the figure's throat, then pivoted low, hooking the back of his knee and dropping him to the floor in a single, brutal motion.

The second lunged fast. Military trained.

Alex barely blocked the punch. The man moved like a ghost aggressive, close-in but Alex was faster. He ducked under a strike, grabbed the attacker's wrist, and flipped him over his shoulder into the metal racks. The server tower shuddered.

Sarah was already yanking the drive out, her work done.

The first man groaned, trying to rise. Nikolai kicked him square in the ribs, then disarmed him with a twist and a shove.

From the corridor came footsteps more.

"East stairwell," Sarah hissed. "Go!"

They sprinted into the corridor, shadows flickering under the low fluorescent lights. An alarm began to whine not the building's, but an internal silent alert system. Manual override. They'd triggered a lockdown.

"They're sealing the floor!" Alex shouted, vaulting a railing and hitting the steps, two at a time.

At the base level, Sarah jammed a bypass chip into the fire escape control panel. Her fingers trembled, but the green light blinked, unlocked.

The door blew open, revealing a loading bay slick with condensation and half-lit by a flickering overhead strip. The space stretched out into the dark, all concrete and echo. Somewhere in the distance, a gate alarm began to wail.

They had seconds.

"This way," Alex hissed, pointing to a narrow corridor that ran between stacked pallets and a metal waste chute. They sprinted across the bay, boots slapping the damp ground, their breath rising in sharp clouds.

Behind them, the stairwell door slammed open again the thud of boots on metal rang out. More Argus personnel. No shouting. These weren't enforcers. They were backup.

"Keep low," Sarah whispered as they ducked behind a stack of crates. The loading doors were sealed. No easy exits.

Nikolai scanned the far end of the bay. "There, catwalk ladder. If we get up to the gantry, we can drop onto the roof over the side annex."

They ran for it.

The metal ladder creaked under their weight. Alex hauled himself up first, then reached down to pull Sarah after him. Nikolai brought up the rear, pausing just long enough to kick the base of the ladder sideways. It folded with a groan, crashing to the floor.

They scrambled along the narrow gantry, breath tight, boots thudding against steel. From the far end of the bay, a red sensor light blinked into life.

"CCTV unit's tracking," Nikolai warned.

One by one, they followed, then sprinted across the rooftop toward a low maintenance ladder descending to the rear alley.

Gunmetal clouds loomed overhead, fat with storm tension. Street sounds drifted up traffic, a bassline thumping from a passing car. But here in the shadows, only adrenaline spoke.

They hit the alley and ran, winding through bins, puddles, the smell of diesel and wet brick filling their lungs.

Alex didn't look back until they were streets away. Then, finally, he let them slow. Heart hammering, breath ragged.

Sarah hunched against a wall, clutching the drive. "one hundred percent… maybe a little less. But enough."

Nikolai scanned the rooftops. "We need to move again. Fast. If they know we got out"

"They do," Alex said. "And they'll be coming."

They slipped back into the streets not ghosts this time, but prey.

And predators always returned to the trail.

Chapter 41: Broadcast Day

The fallout began before the first sip of coffee reached a minister's lips.

A document leak genuine, explosive, landed on the desks of two major UK newsrooms and half a dozen foreign correspondents. It wasn't just any file. It was a high-level security briefing dated six months before John Winters' death. The red stamp read TOP SECRET – DOMESTIC OVERSIGHT SUSPENDED – KESTREL AUTHORITY.

Argus Directive Group was not only operating domestically it was being protected.

MPs scrambled. Civil servants ghosted their own inboxes. A planned media blackout collapsed in hours. Conspiracy threads went mainstream. News tickers pulsed across breakfast TVs:

"Leaked Briefing Links UK Officials to Private Military Network."
"Argus: Rogue Security Group or Government Asset?"

In a dim warehouse loft, the air buzzed with the glow of laptops, hotspot rigs, and a pirate broadcast server that Sarah had built from scratch.

She turned toward the others, her face lit with resolve.

"This is it. The final push."

Alex leaned against the metal shutter, arms crossed, head bowed. "We get one shot."

Sarah tapped in final lines of code. "I've secured time on an emergency override channel, they use it for national alerts. We spoof a system outage. It'll trigger an auto-failover to our feed. Two minutes max, and we'll be *everywhere*."

"But they'll trace it," Nikolai said flatly.

Sarah nodded. "Yes. And this time, they'll know who we are. No masks. No voice changers."

Alex straightened. "We'd be signing our names to it."

"Exactly," Sarah said. "They'll come for us. Fast."

A silence hung in the room, thicker than the tech static.

"I'm in," Sarah said quietly. "They buried John. Burned everything we tried to uncover. If this is how I go out, I go out knowing I didn't stay silent."

Nikolai looked down at the floor, jaw tense. "

He looked up, defiant.

"I'll do it. But on one condition: *you two disappear after this goes live.*"

Alex moved to protest, but Nikolai raised a hand. "This only works if someone survives. If all of us go down, there's no one left to finish it."

Sarah blinked hard, emotion flashing. "Niko…"

He smiled faintly. "Besides, who better to cause a distraction than a ghost from two countries' kill lists?"

Alex stepped forward. "You don't have to do this alone."

"I already am alone," Nikolai said. "But I won't die for nothing."

They set the cameras.

At 18:00, the UK's emergency broadcast network flickered onto all main channels.

Then the screen went black.

Then Sarah appeared.

No background. No edits. Just truth.

"My name is Sarah Lane. I am a former government officer.

I was embedded inside Argus Directive by John Winters.

I didn't know everything at first. By the time I understood, it was too late.

Argus is not just a private military contractor, it is a coordinated system of corruption called "Helix", resource control, and huge political influence.

And it's operating inside the United Kingdom with Government approval."

Then Alex stepped in.

"My name is Alex Winters. John was my father. He died trying to expose this.

And now the evidence lives in our hands and yours. You will find links, documents, transfer files, and video. They are real. Verified. Spread them.

Because if we fall, the truth doesn't."

Nikolai's part was last.

His face was calm. Resolute.

"My name is Nikolai Sokolov. I've fought on both sides of wars and John was my father too.

I've seen what power does when it goes unchecked.

This isn't about left or right, east v West, Britain or Russia. This is about the systems that control your water, your food, your medicine and more importantly you.

"And the men who profit from keeping you in the dark. I will not run from anymore."

They cut the stream.

For two minutes, the UK was forced to listen.

Back at the warehouse, sirens wailed in the distance. Already closing in.

Alex grabbed Sarah's arm. "We go now."

"What about Nikolai?"

He was gone.

A phone lay on the desk, still warm.

On the screen: *PLAY ME.*

Alex hit it.

Nikolai's voice: calm, distant.

"They'll come for me first. That gives you a window.

Finish what we started. And when you tell this story, tell them I chose the truth."

Sarah's voice broke. "He saved us."

Alex nodded once. "Let's make it count."

They vanished into the crowd, leaving only the broadcast and a rising wave of reckoning behind.

Chapter 42: Ashes and Echoes

The streets of Longsight had taken on the weight of knowing too much.

Once noisy, frantic, and alive with the pulse of city breath, tonight they felt stripped of sound. Not quiet. Just hushed, like a city in waiting. As if Manchester itself understood what was about to happen.

Nikolai walked alone, his boots crunching through fragments of glass and damp leaves swept against the curb. The cold mist threaded its fingers into his jacket collar. He didn't pull it tighter. He wanted to feel the air. Wanted to remember what the world felt like when it was just a man and a mission.

He'd left his other phone behind deliberately on a public bench in Crowcroft Park, just beneath the mural of forgotten workers painted across the crumbling walls. A message in itself. Let them follow the trail. Let them find it too late.

In his inside pocket, tucked beneath the lining, was a final drive.
A mirror of the Helix archive.
Encrypted. Distributed. Preloaded with a fail-safe protocol. If he didn't reset the signal within twenty minutes, it would release a cache of data to hundreds of journalists, activists, and whistleblowing platforms. It was a dead man's switch.

He crossed into Garratt Lane, the drizzle turning to a fine sheen. He could see his breath now. It curled up and disappeared into the dark above. Everything about this moment was deliberate.

The mill stood like a carcass against the skyline. Disused. Unlit. Perfect.

He stepped through a rusted doorframe, his footfalls echoing in the wide belly of the old textile factory.

Rain leaked through large holes in the roof, puddling in black pools across the cracked concrete. Long-dead machinery lay sprawled like sleeping beasts. Twisted beams. Rats in the walls.

A place where no one would hear anything. Where no one would interrupt.

He walked to the centre of the main floor and sat on a splintered crate.

Took a breath.

Then another.

From his coat, he pulled a flask.

John's flask. Dented steel, the cap hanging on by a strip of soldered wire.

It smelled like cheap vodka and time.

He drank; let it settle in his throat. Then pulled out the trigger device, an old Soviet signal key rewired into a transmitter. He flipped the switch. A red LED blinked to life:

LIVE FEED – STANDBY.

UPLOAD KEY PRIMED.

He glanced upward.

There was no moon. But he heard it before he saw it.

That distant hum.

Low. Slow. Mechanical.

The buzz of rotors cutting across the damp northern sky.

He didn't flinch.

Instead, he looked up, eyes scanning the rafters and broken windows until he caught the outline.

Drone.

Civilian casing. Survey model. But Nikolai had lived long enough in the East to know better.

The second it repositioned above the broken skylight; he saw the payload compartment.

Too heavy. Too low.

Argus.

He raised the flask again and laughed quietly.

"To endings."

Then, out loud, to no one and everyone:

"You can erase men. But not memory. Not consequence."

A red laser blinked through the dirty skylight.

Target lock.

Nikolai pulled the trigger. Not on a weapon on the drive.

The LED turned green.

UPLOAD IN PROGRESS.

Ten percent. Twenty.

The drone held its position. Waiting for the signal from higher up. The authorisation. It came thirty seconds later, encrypted. From someone they never saw.

KESTREL-APPROVED.

Nikolai didn't look afraid.

He looked... finished.

The drone adjusted one last time.

Not a missile. That was too loud.

Instead: a kinetic shaped charge. Silent. Direct. Surgical.

Impact.

One flash.

The crate was gone.

The man with it.

The entire centre of the warehouse concaved inward, collapsing in on itself like a swallowed breath. Shards of hot steel sizzled in standing water. No smoke. No fire. Just absence.

In Berlin, a freelance journalist received a file flagged *"SOKOLOV."*

In Athens, a dissident tech collective decrypted documents tracing medical supply suppression linked to Argus funding in refugee corridors.

In Bristol, an NHS internal ledger leaked anonymously to a whistleblower:
"Controlled stock restriction: KESTREL INITIATIVE."

And in London, someone very high up in Whitehall threw a chair through a frosted-glass wall and ordered all Helix-related files sealed by executive order.

But it was too late.

The upload had gone global.

Thousands of nodes.

Untraceable.

One message sat at the top of every cache:
"You may kill the voice.
But the echo lives on."
N.S."

In Manchester, Sarah stood in the rain, silent.

Alex stood beside her, eyes on the horizon.

Neither spoke for a long time.

Finally, Alex said, "He didn't flinch."

Sarah nodded. "He never did."

From the far side of the city, the sirens started again.

Not for Nikolai.

Not this time.

For the world he had just lit on fire.

Chapter 43: The Cold Order

The fallout hit like a slow-motion explosion. Every major news outlet ran the leak: *"Helix: The War Economy Hidden in Plain Sight."*
Sarah's voice, clear and clipped, opened the audio file. A confession, a manifesto, and a reckoning.

Video clips of intercepted Argus memos, shipping manifests, washed crypto accounts, MI5 internal redactions. It was all out now, the weapons funnelled through Manchester, the staged scarcity of medical and water supplies, the synthetic inflation of conflict in the East.

And the names.

MPs. Defence contractors. Generals. Editors.

By the next day, five resignations. One suicide. An emergency meeting at COBRA. The Prime Minister refused to comment.

And Sarah Lane, now "traitor" to some, hero to others was a wanted woman.

In an abandoned chapel just outside Sheffield, Alex sat with his back against a stone pillar, staring at the candle Sarah had lit in Nikolai's memory.

He didn't cry. He couldn't.

Not after watching Nikolai make the call, step into the open, and take the drone hit that had been meant for them. It had echoed the blast at Marham. And the one that had taken his father.

Everything circled back. And now it was closing in.

They moved constantly, side roads, burner phones, cash only. Sarah had help from a few old journalist contacts and two former handlers who were now ghosts themselves.

But it wasn't enough.

By Day Four, the digital trail had picked them up again.

The message came at dawn. Delivered not by tech but in paper. A hand-delivered envelope left outside the safehouse in Sheffield.

No stamp. No address. Just a wax seal with a kestrel's claw.

Inside: coordinates.

And a handwritten message.

"Use your father's playbook. We need to talk."

K.

Ten hours later

In a derelict observatory in the Lake District, high on a ridge cloaked in mist, Alex entered alone. Sarah waited outside, armed only with a radio and every ounce of paranoia she could carry.

The inside was stripped bare. Just a single chair. A radio transmitter. And a projector.

It blinked to life.

No face. No name.

Only a voice, low, clipped, British. Ageless and inhuman in its calm.

"You've seen how the world works, Mr. Winters. And how it fails. Your father knew this. That's why he came to me."

Alex stood motionless.

"John thought he could change the system from the inside. But we both knew that was fantasy. You cannot reform a rotting edifice. You dismantle it, piece by piece, and replace it with something functional. Cold. Controlled."

"We are not villains. We are pragmatists. Food, water, medicine these are weapons, just like drones or bullets. Controlled scarcity is the only reliable model in a world of overconsumption and political paralysis."

The screen flashed images, footage from conflict zones, boardrooms, hospitals where water tanks ran dry while Argus stock soared.

"You can burn it all down, Alex. Or you can use it. The files you carry, the names, the routes they're not just evidence. They're tools. The blueprint for a new equilibrium. Not peace. Not war. Order."

A pause.

"Join us. Not as a soldier. As an architect. The long game. It's what your father wanted for you."

Alex's fingers tightened around the Helix drive. The original one. Still partially encrypted. The final layer his father never cracked.

He said nothing.

Only stared at the kestrel symbol projected on the wall.

Outside, Sarah's voice crackled faintly over the radio.

"They're coming, Alex. Choice time."

And inside the observatory... silence.

Alex stood alone, caught between two legacies. One built on truth. The other on power.

And the war, in all its forms, was far from over.

Chapter 44: The Man Behind the Curtain

The hotel room was silent.

Not just quiet, *sealed*. Curtains drawn, phones off, Faraday bags zipped tight. Sarah sat cross-legged on the edge of the bed, decoding the last trickle of data from Nikolai's final upload. The city hummed below them *Salford Quays* all glass and illusion but something irreversible had cracked under the surface.

Nikolai was gone.

Alex hadn't spoken in twenty minutes. He stood motionless at the window, watching the way the light bounced off the canal fractured, blurred, impossible to follow.

Then Sarah's laptop pinged.

Incoming transmission.

Untraceable. Air-gapped. Encrypted so deep it twisted the Helix protocols into a Möbius loop.

Alex moved first. "Run it."

She hesitated. "You're sure?"

"No." He sat. "But run it anyway."

The screen flickered.

Static. Then clarity.

Not a face, a silhouette. Digitally masked. A warbled distortion cloaked every detail, except the voice. Calm. Controlled. British. Educated. *Lethal.*

"You've come far, Alex. Further than John ever managed."

Alex froze.

Sarah's breath caught.

"Don't bother searching the metadata. You won't find me. This isn't surveillance. It's... courtesy."

Kestrel.

The ghost. The architect. The name that haunted every dirty contract and covert memo. Now he spoke as though greeting old friends.

Alex sat forward, eyes narrow. "So you *are* real."

"Real enough. Once Director of Intelligence, before I realised how shallow the roots of power truly were. John and I were students of the same failing institution. He believed in repairing it. I chose to reengineer it."

Sarah's voice was cold. "You turned Argus into a global black market. Weapons, surveillance tech, synthetic famine. You built a war engine."

Kestrel's voice sharpened.

"I restored control. Governments are theatre now. *Actors in suits, reading lines we write.* You've seen it. Members of Parliament laundering through crypto, regulators blackmailed into silence. They're not leaders. They're liabilities. So, I replaced them."

A beat passed. The figure didn't blink.

"Two dozen in Parliament answer to Argus. Two in the Lords sit on my payroll. Three in MI5 still carry out my contingencies. Weak men and women, most of them. But obedient."

Alex swallowed the bile rising in his throat.

"You're admitting this to us why?"

"Because I'm not your enemy, Alex. I'm your invitation."

Silence. The moment hovered like an unsheathed blade.

"John had a vision, scatter light across a broken system. You've inherited something far more valuable: his *playbook.* You know now that power isn't law or legacy. It's *leverage.* You've seen what controlled chaos can achieve. *Now use it.* Join me."

Alex said nothing. He could feel Sarah's eyes on him, searching, wary. The silence stretched.

Then Kestrel added, softly:

"This is your chance to stop fighting *against* the current... and start steering it."

Alex stood slowly. Crossed the room.

"You want me to betray everything my father died for."

"I want you to finish what he couldn't."

Alex's voice turned steel. "He *did* finish it. With a bullet to your system. And a backup that lit the world on fire."

Kestrel didn't flinch.

"And yet I'm still here. The leak hurt us, but not fatally. What you took down was the scaffolding. The foundation's deeper. More... *entrenched*."

Another pause.

"Walk away. I'll clear your name. I'll bury the warrants. Let you rebuild. Or stay in the fire and watch everything you love *turn to ash*."

Alex moved closer to the screen.

"I'm not rebuilding your system. I'm going to bury it."

Kestrel exhaled, almost disappointed.

"Then we are enemies, after all."

The feed cut to black.

Silence returned. Not relief, tension. A coil tightening.

Alex stared at the screen.

"He owns Parliament," he said. "Not metaphorically. *Literally*."

Sarah's voice was quiet. "He turned the state into a front. Now he's trying to turn *you* into a weapon."

Alex shook his head. "He made one mistake."

"What?"

"I'm not my father. But I am his son."

He walked to the window, looking out at the city below. The world that still didn't know it had become a battlefield.

And behind him, Sarah spoke the truth they were both thinking:

Chapter 45: Exit Wound

It started with a whisper.

A message dropped into their ghost inbox the same air-gapped terminal Sarah had built into a busted kettle at the safe flat in Deansgate. The encryption was clean. The metadata scrubbed. No flags.

It read:

"MI5 asset. Code designation: Finch. Defected. Wants to talk. Brings proof of remaining Argus cells. Will only meet Sarah. Location: Canal Street, underpass, 11pm."

Sarah had stared at it for a long time.

Alex was instantly suspicious. "He won't talk to both of us. Not even face to face?"

She shook her head. "It's a lure. But it's not fake. I recognise the code-string. John used to mention Finch. Quiet analyst. Embedded in Signals. Never surfaced after the Helix breach."

"You're not going alone."

"No," she said. "I'm going first."

They had a system now. Flanking overwatch. Shortwave comms. A safe word if things went sideways. She would enter. Talk. Exit. He'd tail the perimeter with eyes high and wide.

But systems don't stop betrayal.

The unlit underpass beneath Canal Street was an echo chamber of footsteps and dripping water. A sickly sodium haze hung under the bridge, old piss, oil slicks, mould climbing walls like rot. Sarah moved calmly, hood up, phone active in her jacket pocket. She scanned left, right. Nothing but shadows.

Then a cough.

From the far pillar.

She turned. A figure stepped out, slight, grey coat, no weapon visible. A man in his fifties, glasses, badly dyed hair, like he still shopped at the MI5 charity ball.

"Finch," she said, without blinking.

"You remember," he answered, with a half-smile. "That's rare."

She kept distance. "You said you had evidence. I'm not here to play trust exercises."

Finch nodded. Reached into his jacket slowly and pulled out a black zip pouch. Dropped it on the concrete between them.

"Flash drive," he said. "Every covert link between Argus and the Joint Committee. Names, bank accounts, contact protocols. It's all there."

Sarah's eyes flicked downward.

Something was wrong.

The air was *too still.*

Then the whisper came, not through her comms, but her instincts. The space behind Finch shimmered, not physically, but *intentionally*. There was something *planted* in this meeting.

She moved back a half-step. "Who sent you?"

"I'm trying to fix a mistake," he said quietly. "But not all of us get to run."

Then he said something she didn't understand. A single word:

"Condor."

And then he stepped back.

And that's when the shot hit her.

No gunfire. Just the crack of impact, *supersonic*. The round punched through her chest like thunder in reverse. Her eyes widened, mouth opening in shock but no scream came. Blood bloomed against her coat.

Alex saw it happen from twenty yards away.

He had been watching from the overpass, eyes locked on her outline. He'd seen the flash, *from above*, not street level. Rooftop sniper. Bolt-action. Suppressed.

She hit the ground hard. No sound. No movement. "SARAH!"

He was already running. Ducking under the railing, boots hammering against concrete. The sniper's position was already cold, clear. Whoever pulled the trigger was already gone. Professional kill.

Finch was gone too.

Alex dropped beside her, hands trembling. "No, no Sarah"

Her eyes fluttered open once. Just once.

She coughed blood. Choked. Tried to speak.

"Tell them…" she whispered. "Not chaos…"

"What? What do you mean?"

"Tell them it's not chaos…" Her fingers closed around his sleeve.

"It's design…"

And then she went still.

He didn't remember how long he knelt there. The blood on his hands was warm, then sticky, then cold.

The pouch sat beside her body.

He took it. Clutched it like a live grenade.

Then the phone in his coat vibrated.

Unknown number.

He answered. Rage bleeding into his voice. "You did this."

Kestrel's voice came through like smoke.

"*You misunderstand me, Alex. I didn't order her death. I allowed it.* There's a difference."

"You're a coward."

"I'm a tactician. Sarah was a liability. You were warned."

Alex couldn't see straight. Could barely hear.

"But it doesn't have to end like this," Kestrel continued. "You can walk away. You have the evidence. Burn it. Trade it. Use it. Join me. We end this war *together* or you die like her, clawing at a broken system."

The line went dead.

Alex stared into the dark.

Two Days Later

The broadcast file from the pouch confirmed everything. Kestrel's control grid. The fake MP appointments in safe seats around the country. Intelligence laundering through private humanitarian fronts. The drone kill orders rubberstamped by *civilian ministers*.

And one final folder. Titled simply: WILLOW.

Inside, a plan.

Stage-managed global destabilisation on the Baltic Coast, food blockades, water scarcity, refugee corridors engineered not to solve crises, but to *trigger them*. The next front wasn't war.

It was *collapse* by design.

Alex didn't run anymore. There was nowhere left to hide and he was going back to London.

Chapter 46: Terminal Orders

London. 03:12hrs.

The city had changed in his absence.

Not visibly the skyline still blinked through the river mist, black cabs still stalked the red-lit corners of Westminster, but something colder threaded the streets now. An invisible pressure.

Alex moved quietly through the shadows beneath the Thames Embankment, he was nervous. The world thought he was dead. Or vanished. The truth, as always, was more complicated.

He reached a maintenance stairwell just past the abandoned Jubilee pier a coded location buried deep in one of John's last files. No guards. No visible security.

But he knew it wasn't unwatched.

He keyed in the access code on the rusted service panel. Four beeps. A hiss of magnetic bolts. Then silence.

Alex descended into the forgotten tunnels beneath London, the underbelly once built for wartime continuity, now repurposed for something murkier.

At the end of the corridor, under corroded lighting and flaking concrete, stood a reinforced door guarded by two plainclothes men with MI5 builds and Argus eyes. One scanned him. The other opened the door.

"Mr Winters," one said. "He's waiting."

The chamber beyond was spartan, clinical all brushed steel and dark glass. One table. One chair occupied.

Kestrel.

Not a man of myth now, but flesh and blood.

Late sixties. Grey suit cut with precision. Clean-shaven. Regal posture, like a man who once stood behind prime ministers, not beside them. His voice was smooth. English upper register. Precise.

"You came," he said, not rising. "Your father would've been proud."

Alex didn't sit. "You killed Sarah. You had Nikolai executed. And you think that's a compliment?"

Kestrel offered a thin smile. "I sanctioned neither. But I allowed both. Your father knew what this would cost. He trained you to accept that, didn't he?"

Alex's fists curled. "He trained me to survive."

"No," Kestrel said, gently. "He trained you to choose."

Alex paced slowly, not taking his eyes off the man. "So, this is it? Your sales pitch? The dragon pulls off the mask and tells me I've been chasing the wrong fire?"

Kestrel stood, finally. Moved to the glass wall, which dimmed and shifted into a high-resolution tactical map not of a warzone, but of London. Supply chains. Utility grids. Food depots. Desalination nodes. Drought contingency routes. Distribution hierarchies.

"You still think this is about politics?" Kestrel asked. "This is about control."

He pointed to the map.

"Water is already monetised. Food is next. The illusion of democracy only survives while supermarkets are full, and taps run clean. That's the lie we maintained. But the state has failed. It is outdated. Sluggish. Bound by legal ghosts. What comes next will not be governed, it will be *managed chaos and civil disorder.*"

"And who does the managing?" Alex asked.

"We do."

Alex took a breath. "You and Argus?"

Kestrel turned. "Argus is a tool. A shell. Just one artery. But yes, we built a new architecture. Not for conquest for stability. The only way forward is controlled chaos. Cultivated breakdowns. Orchestrated repair. That's the war your father finally understood. Before he lost his nerve."

Alex moved closer now. "You mentored him."

Kestrel didn't flinch. "He was the best we ever had. But he couldn't adapt. He believed in 'truth.' In exposure. He thought secrets corrupted. But secrets are *structure*. Secrets are how peace survives blood."

"You destroyed everything he believed in."

"No," Kestrel said calmly. "I offered him a seat at the table. He declined."

A pause.

"And now I offer it to you."

He stepped forward, eyes locked on Alex's.

"Use the Helix files. Control the narrative. You can be the man who guides the chaos. A ghost with a crown. Or... you can continue burning everything and everyone around you in the name of nothing."

Alex didn't move.

Didn't speak.........

03:44hrs — Above Ground

The skyline of London stretched into fog. Parliament lit in skeletal orange. The city buzzed beneath them like a living organism wounded, still breathing.

Alex emerged alone from the access tunnel.

In his hand: a second encrypted drive, offered by Kestrel.

On it: access to backdoors, contingency plans, fail-safes. Insurance.

Behind him: nothing.

Ahead of him: everything.

He stood for a long time near the water's edge, watching the city blink.

The voice of his father echoed faintly in memory.

"You'll have to decide what kind of war you're willing to fight. And who you're willing to become to win it."

Alex slid the drive into his coat.

The rain started again.

He didn't move.

Not yet.

The world had turned, but the centre had not held.

And somewhere, deep beneath Parliament, Kestrel was already planning the next phase.

Epilogue: Afterlight

London hadn't changed. Not in the way Alex had hoped. The flood of revelations had sparked fury, scandal, resignations but no revolution.

Argus dissolved into shadow. Kestrel disappeared like smoke. Parliament scrambled to contain the fallout, patching over the bullet holes with televised promises and inquiries destined to go nowhere.

The headlines changed. The machine did not.

Alex Winters walked now in silence. No more comms. No more allies. Just echoes of voices lost his father, Nikolai, Sarah and the question that gnawed at the edge of every step:

What now?

He could vanish. Disappear into some backcountry of the world with nothing but a name and a fractured past. Or... he could stay in the fight. Not as a soldier. Not even as a whistleblower. But as something else.

The system hadn't collapsed. Not yet.

But maybe next time, he wouldn't play by its rules.

Maybe next time, he'd write the rules.

Thank you for reading Winters Line: Helix Protocol

A father's secrets. A son's war. A system built to destroy both.

If this story moved you, challenged you, or simply kept you turning pages into the night, I'd be incredibly grateful if you could leave a review on Amazon. It helps more than you know.

And if you'd like to see what happens next to Alex — let me know on Facebook. Simon Bywater – Author Page

Because the war isn't over.

It's only changed shape.

Best wishes and keep safe ......

SIMON

Printed in Dunstable, United Kingdom

69034520R00117